Galactic

MW01049477

by Luca Rossi

Contents

Contents   3

Rewind   5

The Kingdom of Turlis   43

Life in Prison   77

Forms of Love   109

Latrodectus Mactans   135

Arcot and the Queen   139

The Perfect Family   155

Maciste   163

Clouded Emotions   171

The Branches of Time   223

The Author   225

Rewind

Jasmine Fantini – May 12, 2013

She's young, beautiful and sensual. She's a star, and for me, unattainable.

I've been following her since the beginning of her career. Showgirl, dancer, singer, actress, hostess…everyone loves Jasmine Fantini. Everything she touches turns to gold.

Blonde hair, baby face, piercing eyes, slightly pronounced lips, upturned nose and disarming smile. Her naturalness and sincerity make her stand out among the jet set. And today audiences are going wild over her.

I'm going to see her. After years of pursuit, I'll soon be close to her. She's having dinner at Il Sicomoro, a restaurant in Piazza San Babila, Milan. About a hundred of us are waiting outside for her.

As soon as news got out about her dining downtown, Twitter went abuzz with guesses on which restaurant she'd be at. The most fashionable places were scrupulously patrolled. Finally *nick73* got a tip from a friend of his, a waiter. He tweeted that he checked his MasterCard balance online, borrowed a jacket and tie from another friend and went to Il Sicomoro, where he sat at a table that cost him a fortune. But just a little while later he was able to post a photo of Jasmine on his Instagram.

She's facing away from the camera, her hair swept back, wearing a silver evening gown and a necklace that looked like it was made from diamonds. The fashionistas tweeted that it was an Armani Privé dress.

After no more than fifteen minutes, the very central Piazza San Babila was crowded with people. The cops, unusually efficient, created a pathway with crush barriers from the entrance of the restaurant to the Bentley parked a few hundred yards away. It could have been parked closer, but Jasmine always said she didn't mind a quick dip in the crowd, since she loved her fans and wanted to feel close to them.

My stomach hurts: I've been squashed against the crush barrier for almost an hour. Everyone behind me has their smartphones ready to take pictures they'll post on their blogs and social networks.

I left my Galaxy in my jacket pocket. No pictures - I just want to see her and feel, if only for a moment, that we share the same air.

It's her. Here she comes. I feel like I'm going to lose it. She seems to be laughing heartily towards her escort, John Artwood, the actor she worked with in her latest Hollywood film. She leans against his arm, giggling. The gesture makes me hate him fervently. Then Jasmine turns to look in front of her. Our hearts stop beating. We hold our breath. For a second the shouts subside to hushed murmurs. Jasmine brings a hand to her lips, then makes a sweeping gesture towards us. She sent us a kiss!

The crowd explodes. Every kind of compliment and declaration of love flies through the air. The cops struggle to keep the crush barriers steady. People are shoving so hard behind me that the pain in my stomach almost takes my breath away.

I see her coming towards us, flanked and followed by photographers. Every once in a while she shakes a few hands that make it over the cop-crush barrier-photographer barricade. She stops to sign a couple autographs. I think she even responds to something someone said. Then she moves on.

She's almost made it to where I stand. If she shakes my hand, if she says so much as a word to me, I don't know what I'll do!

When she's just a few steps away, the two cops in front of me squeeze together. I hold my hand out over their shoulders, but it hits the back of a photographer.

She's right in front of me, but I can't see her anymore.

"Jasmine, I love you!" I tell her with all of the strength I can muster from my body, squashed against the crush barrier.

For a second it seems like she's about to turn around, but she moves ahead a few more steps, stopping to sign another autograph.

Well, she heard my voice, at least. I try to console myself.

I catch a last glimpse of her gorgeous legs as she gets into the Bentley.

I will never forget this moment.

Lightning – August 10, 2014

"When is this crisis going to end? I can't take it anymore!"

Alessio doesn't know how to respond. Pudgy, thick goggles, shirt hanging out of his jeans. He's practically the prototype of a nerd.

We run a rather successful web agency called Starweb. We're expanding our business, and it's been going pretty well, but young entrepreneurs run into lots of obstacles in Italy. The fiscal pressure is unbearable and every day we wind up fighting with the banks over credit limits and loans, not to mention customs agencies and tax collectors.

"If we moved to an emerging country it'd take a lot of work at first, but we'd still get short-term results if we were in a growing economy. And the government wouldn't try to kill us with taxes," I continue.

For years Italy has provided the global example of a nation that massacres entrepreneurs with unfair taxes and bureaucracy. People can't take it anymore. Companies close and start up again elsewhere. The only people left either don't know where to go, are idealists or are lazy. The others try their luck elsewhere.

Alessio and I have been having the same conversation for months.

"Tons of people know us online. Thirty-seven percent of our sales already come from clients outside of Italy. True, things would probably drop off a little here and it wouldn't be easy to serve our old clients once we're abroad, but at least we'd find companies to collaborate with that want to invest and believe in the future. They'd be perfect clients!" I tell him.

Alessio likes the idea as much as I do: we both have friends and contacts all over the world, thanks to the internet. He looks at me sadly.

"Could we bring her along with us?" I immediately regret having suggested the idea.

Grandma!

Alessio lost both of his parents in an accident when he was little. Since then, he's lived with his grandma for practically his whole life. The two are really close and adore one another. She made sure that he didn't miss out on any of the affection his parents would have given him. And now he wants to pay her back any way he can.

Grandma Pina was born in 1930. She's lived in the Porta Vittoria neighborhood forever and couldn't imagine living somewhere else, away from her friends, her café, her usual walks. It's all part of the sweet routine for an elderly lady who, in these very streets, survived the Allied bombing, the roundups by the Germans, a life of hard work and the death of her son, Alessio's father.

Yes, it's true. Alessio can't leave Milan. And I can't leave Alessio.

"Come on, it'll get better. These assholes in the government will understand sooner or later that things can't keep going this way. And besides, we're the best. As soon as the economy gets better, our sales will triple! How about a friendly match of Doom 4?"

A rhetorical question. He adores playing shooter games by Id Software and is even one of the world's best in multiplayer. With me, he's like a cat playing with a mouse. Generally, when I want to make him feel better, I let him exterminate me for a few hours.

Before starting the game on my Dell, I glance at the Facebook page of Jasmine Fantini. I'm one of the 3,248,697 people who like her public profile.

She just posted a photo of herself in Syria.

"At least she was able to make it big abroad," Alessio says, still a little dejected.

Everyone in the world knows Jasmine, but she's originally from a little town near Parma. The Americans think she's the new Sophia Loren. In just a few years, she was able to eclipse other beautiful and famous actresses, like Maddalena Alessi.

She was appointed a UN ambassador and the images in front of my eyes show her helping the Syrian people who've been hit hard by a war that's lasted too long.

While I think about Jasmine, out of the corner of my eye, I notice a strange glow outside of the window.

"Did you see that?" I ask Alessio.

"What?"

"It seemed like a flash."

"Huh?"

"Like a flash in the sky!"

"I didn't see anything!"

"It looked like the sky, for just a second, was all lit up."

"Listen, if you stop wasting bullets, I'll let you take the laser-canon."

"Look, I'm serious here – let's see if there's something about it on Twitter."

In fact, nobody had seen anything.

"Were you smoking something?"

Alessio is a little unnerved. He knows full well that I've never tried any type of drug in my life.

The mouse in my hand seems to be moving on its own. I'm kicking ass. We're at twenty-one to five in Deathmatch mode. That's never happened before.

Our two avatars move around spasmodically searching for one another. I've killed him with every type of weapon. I make the twenty-second kill with three pistol shots to the head, from behind.

"Come on, not the pistol! I can't believe it!" he complains.

I smile at him. I don't know what to say. Even I'm a little surprised.

"Up until now you've won, just barely, the last eight hundred forty seven games!" I declare. "It doesn't seem all that crazy that I'd defeat you every once in a while!"

"Maybe Fantini has a special effect on you?"

The office phone rings. I look at the time on my Galaxy's screensaver. *7:45 pm! Who would be calling this late?*

"Good evening," a low and slightly hoarse voice says. "This is Giorgio De Martinis from Sabauda Bank. Can I talk to Mr. Alberto Ferrari?"

"Of course," I answer. "Speaking."

My heart races. We recently pitched an innovative electronic payment system to Sabauda Bank. It's one of the top five banks in Europe, and if they were interested in our services, we would be able to take the market by storm and introduce the new technology to loads of dealers. It would be a gigantic boon for our little business.

"We've looked over your proposal, and we find it very interesting. Would you be able to come by our office and discuss things further?" he asks, calmly.

"Sure. When would you like to meet?"

"I meant now, actually."

I look at Alessio, who's listening on the speakerphone. He's as incredulous as I am.

"I'll be there in ten minutes."

10

Success – December 15, 2014

Alessio and I had created an innovative payment system based on the biometric data of users. It can be used with any latest generation smartphone. We immediately sent in our patent request, which was approved. We actually weren't entirely convinced that we could sell our invention, but it didn't sound like a bad idea.

Just a few months after we signed the agreement with Sabauda Bank, our invention became the fastest diffused payment system in human history. First the Italians, then their European neighbors got used to buying things in stores and transferring money using smartphones equipped with our app.

All those sleepless nights caused by the economic crisis last summer are but a memory now, and Starweb hires new staff every day, both in Italy and in the other offices that we're opening abroad. We work every day of the week, sometimes all night long.

"I still can't believe that they put their faith in the hi-tech fantasies of two kids," I say absent-mindedly.

Alessio looks up from his PC running on Ubuntu Linux. The thick lenses of his glasses make his eyes look super tiny. "But our idea is revolutionary!"

"True, but banks aren't interested in innovation. They generally take on new technologies years after everyone else does. And then they give the big contracts to people they know, like a company run by some manager's wife. There's no way they could have simply believed in our project."

Alessio is the technological whiz, while I handle the business end of things. He has a hard time understanding how things work in the market. "Anyway, we're in the game now, and with what we're making, we can afford to invest in even more growth."

We're making the transition from a web agency to a software house with interests in different sectors. Sometimes I feel like it's all happening too quickly.

Distracted, I click on the favorites bar of my Google Chrome browser.

Jasmine Fantini's most recent Facebook post is from the set of her latest film. She's the starring actress in a new Hollywood science fiction epic, playing the part of a space explorer. On a planet covered with ocean and no land, she's the only one who believes that a species of intelligent life capable of sending signals into space exists underwater. When she succeeds in making contact with the aliens, not only do they turn out to be highly evolved, but they also help her discover something that will change the fate of the Earth.

In the pictures taken on the set, Jasmine is more beautiful than ever. She wears tight astronaut suits that instantly became a vital fashion *must* among her fans. My eyes linger on the lines of her thighs, her beautiful legs and her perfect derriere.

All of a sudden the notifications icon on Facebook starts going nuts. My Galaxy is receiving new messages at a steady rhythm. *What's going on?*

I read the first messages:

We're with you!

Those blockheads don't understand anything, don't give up!

On the street, police sirens are coming closer.

The doorbell rings.

Alessio, his face as white as a sheet, gets up to answer.

"Police. Open up!"

The world seems to crumble around us. We look at one another, frozen by fear. Neither of us has ever had any problems with the law. We spent our adolescence playing on the computer and our few adult years working. There's no way they're coming here over a few torrent files we downloaded illegally!

I look out the window: six cars with their sirens on have stopped in front of our door.

Without realizing what I'm doing, I hit the tab for Google News. The headline is: new Sabauda Bank payment system has gone haywire. Tens of millions of Euro in damages. CEO Roberto de Medici blames the supplier.

This can't be happening!

The scam – January 3, 2015

The new payment systems Starweb sold to major European banks work perfectly. The only defective systems were the ones used by Sabauda Bank. Starweb engineers spend weeks doing everything they can to help investigators.

The technicians from Sabauda Bank are interrogated over and over. Their phones are tapped. Some of them are taken into precautionary custody and blocked from communicating with their colleagues, managers and family members.

Things get worse and even more stressful: nobody was prepared for such a thorough investigation. The TV news show images of people being brought before the investigators: their faces are tired, pallid and drawn.

In the meantime, our technicians have already discovered inconsistencies between the code we provided Sabauda Bank and the one implemented in the payment systems.

The bank's technicians spill the beans and all that needs to be figured out now is who ordered the modifications.

We finally find out that the bigwigs at the bank requested a few extra lines of code be inserted so that they could record the user's personal data.

Modifications of the source code constitute a breach of contract between Sabauda Bank and Starweb.

When all is said and done, the media descend like vultures upon the bank's cadaver. The damage to their image is colossal. Bank employees at all levels of authority are fired. A historic institution that's been in business for almost two centuries is destroyed in just a few weeks.

On the other hand, our image comes out even better than before. People see us as the millionth victim of a huge banking institution's abuse of power. The blogosphere treats us like we're heroes.

I'm entirely surprised by what just happencd, but also elated: "We can't really complain about how it all worked out. We're free to sell our system to anyone in Italy. And now everyone will buy it! When it was exclusive to Sabauda Bank everyone wanted it. Now they'll have it. In three weeks we'll have over ninety percent of the market for payment systems," I explain to Alessio.

It feels like a dream!

"Unless..." Alessio is pensive. He looks out the office window. Light flurries are falling. A few degrees lower and Milan will wake up with white streets.

We're still in our old office at Lampugnano. We already have branches located in almost every European country, in North America, Korea, Japan and China. The central headquarters were transferred to a fancy Milanese skyscraper. But Alessio and I prefer to work holed up in the two rooms where everything started. We still have the same office chairs, desks and cheap cabinets. I never even really liked them. Only the computers are latest generation and scrupulously maintained.

"Unless what?" I ask him.

"Unless we decide to replace the banks!" he says, smiling how he always does when he's sure he's got a genius idea.

I look at him, perplexed. He continues: "Who believes in banks any more? First the whole mess with the Parmalat scandal, then the derivatives, the 2008 crisis and so on. People don't trust these scumbags in suits and ties anymore. If they could, they'd happily get rid of them. We can present ourselves as something different and innovative, only online. People can transfer their money through electronic wires from their old accounts to Starweb. We'll set up ATMs around the cities for automatic deposits of what little cash remains in circulation. We'll publicize the fact that we're keeping the money without investing it in risky financial operations. What people give us we'll give back as loans, and we'll pay interest with the difference. And most importantly, we'll publish everything – everything that we take in and all investments – online, using the most transparent data possible, something even a kid could understand."

I've always liked Alessio because he's a dreamer like me. And when he's convinced of something, his enthusiasm is both unstoppable and contagious.

Back when we were kids, whenever we found something really beyond our reach, we immediately made it our objective.

I remember one afternoon when we were in the mountains, we got the idea to climb up a gigantic boulder thirty feet high. Without any equipment, we put our imaginations to work. It took us several hours to get to the top. Once we got up there, we were so thrilled you would have thought we had landed on an alien planet.

Unfortunately, we had forgotten to think about how to get down. We were alone in an isolated spot: nobody was around to give us a hand.

We made it back home, all black and blue, as the sun was setting. I'll never forget how my mother and his grandma yelled at us: both were more angry than relieved to finally see us alive.

"Technically it's not impossible," I tell Alessio. "Financially, it's so-so. Politically...they'll shoot us on sight! Here in Italy, when you have an idea that's going to weaken the powers that be, something strange immediately happens to you. It's no secret! The power belongs to the banks. The political parties and the big companies that own the banking institutions control the flow of capital, the economy and the lives of citizens. If we mess around on their territory, we'll be dead before we even get started."

When he has an idea, however, Alessio doesn't give up easily. "Let's do it without them noticing. We'll set up the systems and the technology and sign the necessary agreements. We'll do it as if, even if word gets out, it'll look like it's no big deal. We'll keep a really low profile. Then, when everything is ready, we'll launch it on the internet. We'll put up websites all at once. We'll start with a massive campaign on Google, social networks and YouTube. We'll try to make it as viral as possible. No advertising in magazines, newspapers or TV. We'll work it so that our advertising is entirely done by people themselves. Word of mouth among millions of people should do the trick."

"Alessio, this time we're sticking our tongues out at the big boys, you know that, right?" I say, still doubtful.

He smiles, since he knows me too well. He knows I'm already in.

"They'll do everything they can to trip us up," I continue. "In the end, we'll probably risk an important market, like the Italian market. Ok, let's do it!"

Sorgente Bank – June 16, 2015

Office of Stefano Pellini, CEO of Sorgente Bank.

Micro-camera placed on the file cabinet facing the desk.

Giorgio Bertuzzi, Managing Director of Sorgente Bank, seen from behind: "We're losing millions."

Stefano Pellini, CEO of Sorgente Bank: "Give me the data, Giorgio!" in a dry and annoyed tone.

G.B.: "Stefano, we've never seen anything like it. The situation has already gotten worse since I printed this out for you. And it's getting bleaker as we talk."

S.P.: "What is this *Star Bank* all about?"

G.B.: "It's those guys from Starweb, the ones who've covered half the world with their biometric wireless payment systems. They broke their contract with Sabauda Bank six months ago over that mess about collecting user data, and just today they launched their own bank."

S.P.: "So there are actually people willing to put their own money in the hands of these ragamuffins?"

G.B.: "People? It's a mass phenomenon. It's all you can read about on the internet right now. Typical sentence: *I took all of my money away from the loan sharks. Enough with dirty finance.* They started spreading stories on the derivatives, loss of funds and speculation. People are flooding us with messages saying they don't trust us anymore and can't wait to get away from us."

S.P.: "Stefano, are you a little boy? Nobody believes the internet! Call the heads of the papers and the TV news, let's clarify how things really stand."

G.B: "Giorgio, it's 2015! People buy things on the internet, make friends on the internet, trust what they read on the internet. If millions of users give you advice, you'll do what they tell you to. And nobody's listening to the experts on the TV news since they're all playing with their little tablets while they're watching the show!"

S.P.: "Okay, okay, leave me alone here, I'll take care of it."

Giorgio Bertuzzi leaves the room.

Stefano Pellini dials the number 06 4530***.

Augusto Baldecchi, Channel 1 producer, responds.

A.B.: "Hello?"

S.P.: "Hi, it's Stefano. How's it going?"

A.B.: "Crazy. Insane. The usual."

S.P.: "Listen, did you already pull something together on *Star Bank?*"

A.B.: "Something...everyone seems to be nuts about it on the internet. How's it going for you? I read that your stocks are falling in the exchange."

S.P.: "Ah, well, it's just speculation! We haven't even lost a single Euro. Everything you read is trash."

A.B.: "You really think so? Everyone's writing about how they've closed their old accounts and are going to *Star Bank.*"

S.P.: "Maybe they closed the accounts they had with the little banks in the middle of nowhere. But nobody would leave Sorgente Bank for those guys."

A.B.: "Ah, okay."

S.P.: "Listen, I need to tell you something so you can get prepared. But for now, please, this remains between us. You can tell everyone and their mother about it later. Listen: Star Bank is running on borrowed time!"

A.B.: "But it just got started!"

S.P.: "Sure, but do you know how it got started?"

A.B.: "Uh...I read that they prepared everything in secret for six months and then came out like a rocket."

S.P.: "Yeah, sure, but the money?"

A.B.: "They probably don't have big problems with liquidity: they sell wireless payment systems over half of the globe."

S.P.: "Are you kidding? Listen. We're advisors to some of their associated companies, we know their books: they're losing across the board. The classic scenario, debt buried in a few thousand companies in fiscal paradises, you know...completely unmonitored, and everything looks like it's oozing with liquidity, but they don't have a Euro in the bank."

A.B.: "Okay, but the Bank of Italy, the tax authorities...nobody knows about this?"

S.P.: "Well they do have a few Euro, but it's not theirs."

A.B.: "Whose is it?"

S.P.: "Laundered money."

A.B.: "They must be crazy! So they're already dead!"

S.P.: "But you don't know who's involved! It's the Mafia. Billions of Euro..."

A.B.: "No way! It's the story of the year! Is there anyone else who knows?"

S.P.: "Nobody."

A.B.: "We're on it!"

S.P.: "Destroy them for me, ok?"

A.B.: "No need to ask."

S.P.: "Listen, that girl who does the evening news, is she in the game?"

A.B.: "When should I send her to you?"

S.P.: "Tomorrow. But to the apartment in Rome, tomorrow at 4pm. Have you tried her out?"

A.B.: "Of course, she's dynamite in bed!"

S.P.: "Great, we'll talk later and you can tell me what you've come up with."

A.B. "Bye!"

The conversation ends.

Stefano Pellini dials 02 3949***.

Lucio Badalucchi, public prosecutor, responds.

L.B.: "Yes?"

S.P.: "Hi, it's Stefano."

L.B.: "Oh, hi, Stefano. You don't need to say anything, I know you're right! You'll have to forgive me but I haven't really started the inquiry on the Morini brothers. We've been swamped with new files and it's taking all of our staff away."

S.P.: "Don't worry. In any case nobody will be at the little haven in August. Listen, you need to check out something pretty big for me ASAP. You'll end up on the TV news all around the world. But when I say ASAP, I mean there's not a minute to waste."

L.B.: "Fire away."

S.P.: "Ok, do you know those guys from Starweb? Today they launched a dirty little bank on the internet. It's really nothing, just a way to steal the savings of a handful of losers. But the scandal that's about to come out is how much money the Mafia has given them. Before someone else gets a hold of this news, I think it'd be best for you to take care of it, right?

L.B.: "No question about it. We'll get right on it!"

S.P.: "Great, but there's a problem. I need a notice of investigation before tomorrow."

L.B.: "No, we can't do that. Alessandro's going to the opera tonight. We can't do anything without the magistrate."

S.P.: "You just need a signature?"

L.B.: "Right, the rest I can take care of. We can make it look like the inquiry started two months ago. We'll throw together a little documentation, I'll send something to myself by police mail. Anyway we're sure to find some Mafiosi that know them over the internet."

S.P.: "But where do you get that kind of information?"

L.B.: "Stefano, are you still living in the stone age? Anyone can see who's following you on social networks. Someone like Obama has forty-five million followers on Twitter. The Google guys have fifteen. The kids at Starweb should have a couple million. You think we wouldn't be able to find the name of someone with ties to the Mafia among so many followers? All we need is a few messages exchanged. Then it'll be up to them, some time later in the future, to prove that they didn't mean to say what they wrote."

S.P.: "Bravo, bravo! If you go after them for laundering dirty money, they'll disappear in the blink of an eye."

L.B.: "Don't worry, we'll take care of them. Nobody will remember them in two months."

S.P.: "Ok, keep me in the loop."

L.B.: "As always! And don't forget about the favor, my wife wants to go to Bora Bora this year."

"Enough, I can't take it anymore! These guys make me vomit. Can you believe this? Bank tycoons, TV directors, the prime minister, magistrates...they higher up you go, the more corrupt they are!" Alessio is reading the wiretaps published in the newspapers this morning.

Since Sabauda Bank disappeared six months ago, its main competitor, Sorgente Bank, thought it was omnipotent. The birth of Star Bank caught them unprepared, as we thought it would.

"I told you they'd come after us any way they could. *Hit hard, hit fast.* That's how these people think. We got off easy here. If Stefano Pellini wasn't being tapped, he probably would have massacred us," I respond.

"No, he wouldn't have gotten us. We don't know anyone in the mafia!" Alessio protests.

"Look, Pellini wasn't exactly wrong: we don't need to go to lunch downtown with the Mafia every day in front of everyone else. All he needed was for it to *seem* like we knew them and they could cover us in mud all they wanted. Anyway, an investigation in Italy takes twenty years. Maybe in the end you could prove your innocence, but what good would it be then?"

"At least I'd be reimbursed!"

"Yes, by the government, not by the people who put you under investigation. They'd get off scot-free. So in the meantime they've already finished up their brilliant careers and started enjoying a fantastic pension."

"All of this just makes me sick to my stomach."

I should feel relieved that we escaped danger, but I can't relax. I feel that something is still wrong, but I can't figure out what.

"Listen, Alessio, do you ever get the feeling that things are going a little too well for us?"

I realize my words are absurd, but I feel really strange thinking about how things worked out.

"Too well? Every time we turn around there's another mess!" Alessio retorts.

"Sure, but think about it for a moment. Every time something bad happens, not only do we come out the winners, but we come out even stronger than before."

"If anything, that just means we know how to take advantage of every opportunity," Alessio responds.

"You're right, but are we really that good? We have some good ideas, of course! But there are a lot of people out there who are smarter than us who would come out much worse!"

"Maybe we're better at putting our ideas into practice. Look at Apple with the first iPhone. For years, they just copied everyone else's ideas. Nokia had launched smartphones with touchscreens a few years earlier, and they were horrible. But the iPhone became a must. It's not enough to have good ideas, you need to master their implementation."

I'm not all that convinced. I still feel that something weird is going on. But I let it go: Alessio had been under a lot of stress over the past few weeks, and now that he's finally feeling more relaxed, I don't want to give him more to worry about. And not even I (fully) understand what's behind this bizarre feeling.

We track the numbers of our new creature over the next few days, completely amazed. Star Bank racked up some impressive numbers pretty quickly. The mangers we hired are working nonstop to keep up with all of the requests.

What's most surprising, though, is the climate of collaboration created with account holders. The transparency we based our bank on generated unlimited trust from our customers.

The interview – September 11, 2015

"We're back now with our guest Alberto Ferrari, CEO of Starweb. Alberto, I think we'd all like to have a fairytale career like yours: you started off with a small web agency and now you run a global IT giant, with branches in several new sectors. But things aren't going so well for everyone else in our country. The crisis doesn't seem to be ending anytime soon and many people are losing faith in the solutions proposed by politicians. We're in the thick of campaign season, only two more months until elections. What do you think of the candidates and what do you expect from them?"

It's Sunday afternoon, and I'm in the Channel 1 studios being interviewed by Maddalena Alessi. I remember thinking, when I used to watch TV, that studio stages were much bigger than what they are in reality. It's really hot, but nobody except for me seems to be suffering.

Alessi is splendid. She's wearing a very short red dress with a plunging neckline. Her copper hair is styled in long ringlets, a style that recently came back into fashion. She nonchalantly shifts in her chair, as if she was in her own living room.

I try to take my eyes off of her crossed legs: I really shouldn't leer like a creep in front of millions of viewers.

I think about Jasmine Fantini. *Too bad she's not interviewing me!* It's not that Alessi isn't cute, Jasmine is just from a whole other planet. But she's not working as an anchorwoman anymore, and she's almost always in the United States.

Okay, concentrate on the question: politics!

"I'd rather not talk about individual candidates. I think that our country has enormous potential. Everyone would agree on that point. But it's difficult to be successful..." I start to say.

Maddalena interrupts me: "It seems to me you've figured that out."

"True, but we've been really fortunate. People trust us, and not everyone has that kind of luck. It's difficult to work in Italy with all of the bureaucracy and taxes holding you back. This pushes a lot of people out of the country. When somebody leaves, the country grows weaker. I believe that this vicious cycle needs to be broken."

"That sounds like the sort of thing everyone is saying these days."

"Yes, and in fact I think everyone can clearly see what needs to happen. But whoever gets elected will probably start paying more attention to their own interests than the public's interest. And then people always try to cover up what they're really doing, which of course the public doesn't like."

"So what would you do?"

"Well, for example, when we decided to create Star Bank, we based it on a simple idea: complete transparency. Today anyone can go online and download any type of data on any sector of our business. Sure, this might make it easier for our competitors to copy us, but our customers like it. They know exactly what's working and what could be done better. Most of all, they know what we're doing with their money."

"And do you think this could be applied on the national scale?"

"Of course! We all know that politicians use our money in really shady ways. Look at what we've done with Star Bank: you can make a sort of analogy with how the government should work. Whoever logs in online should be able to understand in a clear and unambiguous way what topics are being discussed, where the public money is going and why. Then voters would stop allowing the nation's budget to get eaten up by a thousand side interests. Politicians would be required to release billions of Euro in resources that were previously used the wrong way."

"You don't think your point of view is a little too idealistic?"

Her chestnut eyes shine, reflecting the studio lights. Her words flow freely, breezily. I start doubting that my rant was very convincing. Actually I've never really been much into politics. Maddalena is probably right: it's not that easy to implement the ideas I was going on about once you get mixed up in the complex logic of politics.

"You're probably right, Maddalena, but that's at least what I would try to do."

"I'd recommend that you don't say it too loud, unless you want to find your Twitter flooded with the hashtag *#AlbertoForPresident.*"

"Don't worry, Maddalena, I've already had enough excitement with a couple banks this year. I'd say that's enough for now."

"Thank you, Alberto, for taking the time to visit with us. We're happy to have role models like you out there to inspire young people who want to create successful businesses."

"Thanks for having me."

"Now for the latest sports news, let's go to the soccer fields and see how the Sunday games are going..."

While Maddalena introduces the sports news, I get up and head towards the exit. Away from the video cameras, I stop to watch the dancers get ready to go on stage after the sports news. As the segment airs, I lock eyes again with Maddalena.

"Later," she gestures with her hand.

She really is beautiful live.

Elections – December 10, 2015

"Shhh, Alberto, not so loud!" Alessio protests, annoyed because I'm bouncing a ball against the wall.

The big LCD screen shines a blue light on his face, which is focused on the figure of Maddalena Alessi.

"Come on! Turn that stuff off, it makes me anxious!" I reply.

"Really? Alessi does something more than make me anxious. She's ridiculously hot."

"We're live now at the Ministry of the Interior, where the Star Party has jumped to fifty point four percent of voter preference, with ninety percent of polling stations surveyed," announces Maddalena, radiant, on Channel 1.

For me, the news is like a punch in the stomach.

"I can't believe we're winning an electoral campaign run entirely on the Internet!" I exclaim, incredulous.

I still don't understand why I let myself be convinced to get involved in the electoral circus.

After the interview with Alessi two months ago, thousands of people asked me to join the race as a candidate.

For weeks, I refused interviews and public or TV appearances. I finally explained on my blog why I didn't think I was the right person for that role, with the opposite result of creating incredible anticipation that I would indeed enter the race.

But then I began to understand what my candidacy would mean to people: hope. I read thousands of messages from people who saw me as a beacon of hope for the future, for themselves and for their children, messages from people who wanted to go back to having a government they could believe in, people who needed me to once again feel proud of their own country.

I tried to resist, but in the end the people's will got the better of me and I entered the ring.

We decided to create a party, the Star Party, and make no compromises.

Every meeting among management was broadcast through Google+ Hangouts. People debated with us, gave us suggestions and helped us grow.

Every Euro used in the electoral campaign was traced, and the data was published online.

Candidates were placed under the scrutiny of the online community and anyone could express their own opinion.

People participated en masse and the results were surprising. Everything was discussed, created and improved in plain daylight.

Although TV appearances where reduced to the absolute minimum, every candidate in the party accepted debates continuously on a wide variety of media platforms, either with opponents or with the public. For our candidates, it was like playing on home turf. Most of them started out with a thorough understanding of new forms of communication, while the majority of their opponents hobbled along pretending they knew how to use these technologies while they were actually trying to figure out what they were.

We refused any alliance with traditional parties, aware that this would probably lead us to defeat.

The Star Party was modeled along the exact same principles that we proposed to use in the country's government. Alessio, increasingly excited, moves his eyes between the TV screen and the computer display.

He interrupts my contemplation, bringing me back to the present moment: "Alberto, try to focus, you're winning the 2015 elections!"

"Alessio, if I do win, it'll be a joint victory. *I* won't be the winner, *we'll* be the winners!"

"Yes, but you're the one who gets to be the new prime minister in Palazzo Chigi!"

"You're not going to just walk away from this scot-free."

"But who'll stay in cold Milan to run the company while you enjoy the warm weather in the capital?"

"But who will lead the country into the future?"

"The one who was screwed over live on TV by Alessi!"

"Come on, you know I didn't even know what I was talking about! I was trying to stare at her legs without anybody noticing and then I got distracted."

"Bravo! A real genius! Now go tell that to sixty million citizens!"

"We have the definitive information here. Ladies and gentlemen, this is surely a landmark day in the history of Italy. The Star Party, a party that didn't even exist a few months ago, has won the absolute majority of votes in Parliament. The head of state will give Alberto Ferrari the job of creating a new government. Let's go to the headquarters of the Star Party, where they're telling us that the prime minister elect is not yet available for interview. Knowing him, we'll probably get a tweet pretty soon."

"Alessio, please, turn it off."

"Ok, ok!"

Alessio gets up and comes over to hug me. I like the idea of him running Starweb for a while. He's grown up a lot over the past few years and I'm sure he'll figure out how to deal with the sharks in the market without compromising what we stand for.

"And now what?" he asks me. "Time to face the crowd?"

I look at my Galaxy. I have a few tens of thousands of mentions on Twitter.

"@AlbertoForPresident is this the end of the Second Republic?" @goblinta asks me.

"@goblinta, it's the end of the Italy of political parties. It's the beginning of YOUR republic," I respond.

Capri – January 5, 2015

"Alberto, Maddalena Alessi on line three."

"Thanks, Anita."

I'm in Palazzo Chigi, the seat of the President of the Council of Ministers of the Italian Republic.

I got rid of most of the furniture and spruced up the presidential office a little so that I'd feel more at home. I hung a few works of contemporary art that I liked on the walls. I cleared off the desk, leaving just the screen of my Dell, sometimes joined by a tablet and a smartphone. It helps me feel a little less uncomfortable.

A few days after my inauguration, I won the toughest battle yet: convincing Anita Pellegrini, my new secretary, to call me Alberto, not Mr. President. In Italy, titles carry a certain weight.

"Good morning, Ms. Alessi. I believe I haven't had the chance yet to thank you personally for ruining my life. How are you?"

"*Maddalena,* please! We can be a little less formal now," she responds in a sweet tone of voice.

"Okay, Maddalena. How do you feel about changing the history of a nation with just one interview?"

"I'd say rather well. See, despite your lack of faith, TV still has a following."

"I can't say that you're wrong. Anyway, I don't know how to thank you for all that you've done for me, even if it still hasn't really sunk in."

"You could accept my invitation, Alberto."

"Your invitation? To where?"

"Although you've already started cutting all the transportation expenses, do you think you could find a way to get to my villa in Capri one of these evenings?"

"I think so. I can use my personal means of transport, like everyone who preceded me should have been doing over the last seventy years."

"Ay yi yi, you're getting to be so boring! Just a few days in Palazzo Chigi and you're already talking like a politician."

As the quiet electric vehicle travels down the tiny street leading to Maddalena's house, I look at the splendid sunset over the sea surrounding Capri. The Roman emperors used to come here to enjoy the singular beauty of this island. In the back of my mind, I remember that I, too, am now a powerful man. The mere idea makes me feel uneasy.

The gate automatically opens when I'm just a hundred feet from the villa. She probably saw me coming from the surveillance cameras mounted on the surrounding wall, protecting the diva's privacy.

Her mansion is built in a modern style with materials that are traditionally found on the island. Mostly white, it still fits in naturally with the landscape.

The vehicle stops in front of the main gate, then silently starts up again. I observe, astonished, that all of the villa's windows are illuminated, but the lowered curtains prevent me from seeing what's happening inside.

I walk across the gravel driveway and go up the stairs to the entrance. A butler appears next to the front door.

I've never gone to high society shindigs or jet-set parties and I feel slightly out of place. For weeks, I repeated over and over during the electoral campaign that a position in government wouldn't change me, and I wonder if traveling to this island is already a step in that direction.

"Good evening, Mr. President. Ms. Alessi is waiting for you in her private study," the butler tells me.

The house is impeccably decorated: subtle colors, lots of beige, dark furniture, pictures on the walls and lots of niches with both modern and antique statues. Everything seems carefully designed and planned, down to the tiniest details. Right now Alessio is probably playing Doom 4 in our office full of faux-wood plastic furniture. For a minute, I entertain the idea of turning around and taking a plane back to Milan.

The butler leads me down a long corridor to a wide set of French doors with smoked glass panes set inside of dark wood frames. After opening the door, he politely invites me to enter.

"Albert, you're finally here!"

"Hi, Maddalena."

I immediately remember that I'm talking to a star: even in private, she dresses and acts like she's in front of the camera. Her shoes, with astronomically high heels, are black like her dress, which is slit down the side and highlights her beautiful legs. An elegant pearl necklace lies across Maddalena's neckline. Her hair flows down to her shoulders, framing her long face, and the copper color matches her lipstick.

She's splendid. I realize I'm standing, frozen, staring at her. She comes towards me, oozing confidence, puts both her hands on my shoulders and gives me a double kiss hello.

She makes each gesture as if she's playing a character on TV. She's gorgeous, but I think she's in a completely different league than an ordinary guy, the kind of everyday person you'd see on the street. I think about Jasmine again, who seems completely natural in everything she does.

"I hope that the trip from Rome to Capri was pleasant."

"Yes, it was fine, thanks."

"The presidential means of transportation was comfortable?"

I laugh, knowing that she's provoking me.

"I never would have used anything official to come to your place, Maddalena."

"Alberto, everyone falls prey to the pleasures of power. There are some things that even the president of a multinational company can't have until he gets into politics."

"I don't think I'm going to find out what those things are."

"You'll want to soon enough. As time passes, the fascination of being able to make a lot of things go your way will eventually seduce you, as it does with everyone else. You're not the first billionaire to get into politics."

"Your words sound like a challenge...or a threat," I respond.

"Don't worry about it. Powerful men don't have many true friends, but you'll learn to trust me. So, shall we go have a drink with the other ladies?"

The other ladies? I have no idea what she's talking about, but she's already turned around and started walking towards a door on the other side of the study, away from the entrance. I hurry up to follow her down another corridor, elegant and refined like the first.

As we walk along, a side door suddenly opens and two smiling girls come out. They're both very young. The first has smooth brown hair down to her shoulders. The second has a blonde bob. They're wearing nothing but their panties. I'm flabbergasted.

"Alberto, do you remember Cecilia and Giusi?"

I look at the three women in front of me: Maddalena in her

30

skyscraper heels and the two barefoot girls, the brunette leaning on the blonde's shoulder.

My silence must be embarrassing them. They look at one another, a little confused. Maddalena, on the other hand, is cool and collected. My awkwardness seems to amuse her.

"Hi...um, no...actually I don't remember them."

"Alberto, the dancers from Channel 1! I thought you were looking at them when you left our studio."

"Ah, sure, right! Sorry, that was a few months ago."

What a way to go: the head of state, paralyzed, his mouth open in front of two young dancers from TV. Maddalena interrupts my thoughts: "I'm sure you'll remember one person here today, at least. Come on, let's go say hi to the girls."

"After you, Mr. President," the blonde says. She must be Cecilia.

"Please, after you!" I reply, motioning for her to go first instead.

Walking in front of me, they exchange a few whispers and start giggling. Nude, they look like two Greek nymphs. The memory of Roman emperors comes back to my mind.

Before I understand what's happening, and without taking my eyes off the two girls' butts, we enter a gigantic room.

Giusi says hello to a girl that comes towards her, kissing her on the lips. I don't have enough time to look at how incredibly beautiful this new one is before Maddalena distracts me, saying: "Girls, President Ferrari!"

I look up. Behind her, a rather large space is cluttered with the most beautiful female bodies I've ever seen.

Orgy

The room is huge, full of blood red sofas and chairs, white ottomans, dark wood tricliniums with light colored cushions, carpets, curtains, tapestries on the walls, famous pictures, statues. My eyes see everything and nothing. I can't mentally process anything except for the girls.

The first three I notice are on a sofa near us. Two are passionately kissing each other while the third has her lips on the breasts of one of them. I think I saw them on the day of the interview, but I'm not sure.

A little further along, a girl is kneeling on the carpet with her hands tied behind her back, her body and face pressed against the sofa. She's dressed like a waitress, her skirt raised as she's spanked by two dominatrixes wearing black latex suits. The girl's butt cheeks are red. She squeals after she receives each lash.

Girls are sipping champagne on the other sofas, chatting and laughing, indifferent to what's happening around them.

The dress code is rather unique. Almost all of them are just wearing panties. A few are wearing short, colored dresses. No one is wearing a bra.

A little further back, a girl holding a fashion magazine in one hand shows a page to her friend while playing between her thighs with the other hand.

There's a second part of the room, towards the back, up about three steps. It's a smaller, more private space full of large round beds.

On one of these, I see a girl on her hands and knees, blindfolded. Her partner is fucking her with a strap-on, a belt attached to an artificial penis.

Two girls are lying down on the second bed, facing one another, sharing a plastic dildo that's long enough to satisfy them both at once. Their moans are just barely audible from where I'm standing.

After we enter, a few girls get up to come say hello. Others are obviously too busy and don't even notice we're there.

"Hi!", "Hello Mr. President!", "President Ferrari, you're finally here.", "Aren't you hot wearing all those clothes?", "President, I'm Caterina, do you remember me?", "Hello Mr. President, I'm so pleased to meet you."

I try to remember names and faces and babble something in

response.

Maddalena is clearly amused by my confused state, but saves me from embarrassment and invites me to come have a drink with her.

I settle into a corner of the room and pour myself a flute of champagne.

"I hope you're not offended by my little surprise, are you?"

"No, but...it wasn't what I was expecting."

"It's a privilege reserved for powerful men. You can spend some time with interesting people here."

"They work with you?"

"Some do. Others are my friends. And others are friends of my friends."

"And this party is...?"

"It's for you, naturally!" Maddalena interrupts.

"For me?"

"Sure. It may look like we're a bunch of lesbians, but we're all strictly bisexual."

Maybe she was waiting for me to reply, but I couldn't think of anything to say.

"Don't worry. We don't expect you to satisfy all of us," she adds, mischievously.

"But...I really -"

"You really can do and have who you want, and you've got all night long," she continues in a serious tone of voice. "And if you like it here with me, you can come back any night you want. You can whip them or let them whip you. You can let them walk all over you. You can fuck three at once, or five, or as many as you want. You can tell them what you want them to wear or ask them for hot little shows or stripteases. You're the president, nobody will deny you anything."

Despite everything, I start to calm down and regain control over my thoughts. "Maddalena, why did you think all of this would interest me?"

She laughs heartily. "Ah, really? You know, I did suspect that might be the case. Manuel!"

A door opens and a tall, muscular man enters. He has smooth, long hair down to his shoulders and reminds me of a dancer I once saw on TV, but his unusual outfit thwarts my attempt to identify him: he's completely naked.

As he comes towards me, a few girls glance over at him, admiringly.

"Hi Manuel, I'd like to introduce you to President Ferrari," Maddalena says.

"Hello, Mr. President. It's truly an honor."

He comes and sits with us, crossing his legs. I'm more surprised than ever. He has a great body and I honestly didn't expect to find a naked man sitting in front of me.

Maddalena notices my hesitation. "Alright, so we've discovered President Ferrari's weakness here. Manuel, unfortunately, is only gay, which makes it a little less interesting for some of us. But we love having him at our parties."

The showgirl's eyes first study Manuel and then my face, looking for confirmation.

"Manuel," I say, "I hope I didn't disturb you from what you were just doing. In fact, Maddalena and I were just discussing a few things. Could you give us a few minutes?"

"Of course, Mr. President. I don't mind a little bit of privacy myself. If you want to come see me later, we can get comfortable and relax a little," he replies.

He gets up and confidently saunters towards the door he came in from.

"Maddalena, I'm not gay!"

She lifts her eyebrows and takes a sip of champagne.

I continue: "I wasn't trying to tell you I was gay. I actually wanted to ask you something else. Why did you think I would want to participate in an orgy?"

Rather then answer, she gets up, comes and sits closer to me and traces one of her fingernails over the top of my ear.

"I'm happy you're not gay, you know that?"

"Maddalena!"

"Alberto, the answer is simple: because you can. And now you can have what everyone else wants."

"Why did you do all of this for me?"

"Because otherwise someone else would do it, and I don't want to be beat at this game. I worked hard to get to where I'm at. I made a lot of sacrifices. I suffered. But who makes the decisions on Channel 1? Who chooses who goes on the air and who doesn't, who gets the prime time slot and who goes on in the morning to an audience full of housewives? You know it better than I do. The answer is: you politicians! I want to stay where I am, I don't want to lose anything I've worked so hard for and I'm ready to do anything to solidify my alliance with you."

"Maddalena, my politics are different..."

"You go on ahead with your politics during the day, but let me take care of your nights. We can do whatever you want, whenever, wherever and however you want."

"Thanks, but..."

The butler silently appears at the door.

"Madame, Ms. Fantini is here."

Another guest

Boom! I think I skipped a couple heartbeats.

Peeking out from just one step behind the butler, Jasmine Fantini looks at us, amused. She's wearing a white dress with a flowing skirt down to her knees. Her face is pure and angelic, as it always looks. I feel like her childish green eyes are looking right through me. It's the first time I've ever felt Jasmine's eyes on me.

She comes towards us. Maddalena gets up to greet her, but I'm still sitting down, frozen. I realize how impolite this is as Jasmine hugs Maddalena. I suddenly get up.

"President Ferrari, I presume," she says with an ironic smile, before Maddalena can introduce us.

The other girls' eyes are all on her. It's obvious that Jasmine is a mythical figure around here: the actress who works in the Olympia most of them dream of getting to one day.

Jasmine and Maddalena sit down. Again I follow a few seconds behind. I wonder if Jasmine usually goes to these parties. And what kind of relationship does she have with Maddalena? Jasmine seems to be wondering the same things about me: "It's nice to see you haven't lost any time getting familiar with your surroundings, Mr. President," she taunts.

"Jasmine, Alberto kindly accepted my invitation to keep us company tonight as a way of thanking me for my interview back in September."

"Ah, yes, I remember. The interview that led to an electoral campaign based on the concepts of transparency and honesty, among other things," Jasmine said.

"Jasmine is a dear friend of mine, but she loves to get a rise out of people," Maddalena says. "Don't worry Alberto, the girl barks, but she doesn't bite."

"Maddalena," Jasmine explains, "helped me a lot when I was just starting out with my career, when nobody knew who I was. I love her like a sister. But I'm not crazy about her way of handling public relations."

"Jasmine, I just got here." It's the first thing I ever say to Jasmine Fantini and I can't believe that it's an attempt to justify myself.

"That's odd," she responds. "I get the feeling that you're pretty comfortable here."

36

She looks around. Some girls are pretending to do something else and others are watching us attentively. Still others have picked up where they left off.

"Jasmine, don't be so mean to the President. Look how embarrassed he is! Be nice, now, come here."

Maddalena presses against her and kisses her tenderly on the lips. Their kiss makes the blood boil in my veins.

"I'm so annoyed by these politicians who, as soon as they get an ounce of power, think the world is at their feet," she whispers into Jasmine's ear, knowing that I'm listening.

And I'm still stunned by the kiss she just gave her. "Jasmine, look, I..."

Maddalena, seeing how flustered I am, suddenly understands that her friend means something to me.

"Jasmine, Alberto didn't know anything about my little treat. He just found out about it fifteen minutes ago. Right before you got here, he was actually telling me that he wasn't interested in spending time with my girls."

Jasmine's face relaxes. She leans back against the sofa, crossing her legs. She smiles, again amused.

"A gay President of the Council? Did you already introduce him to Manuel?"

Again!

"Jasmine, I'm not gay and I perfectly understood what Maddalena was trying to offer me. Maddalena, thank you, I'm really tempted by your offer. You're not going to get any help from me, but you can rest easy knowing that nobody else is going to get any help to unfairly take away everything you've worked for. I believe that it's up to the people to decide and, even if there are experts on the subject, political discussions and decisions need to be made publicly accessible to all. Enough sneaking around and clientelism. I've already explained in every way possible that, during my presidency, the power will return to the hands of the people."

As I speak, Jasmine looks at me admiringly, and this gives me confidence. I continue explaining what I started to do since I got into the government and how I want to go forward. From the way everyone else is looking at me I realize that I've raised my voice. The dominatrixes have stopped, the waitress turned around. It's an audience I'm not used to, but Jasmine's eyes make the words fly out of my mouth.

When I stop for a little pause, Maddalena applauds, satisfied. "Bravissimo, Mr. President. Now I understand why so many people voted for you."

My eyes are still on Jasmine, who lowers her gaze, maybe because she feels bad about the way she was trying to badger me.

"I'm sure you can forgive Alberto, my dear Jasmine. Given that you were willing to spend sixteen hours on a plane without even knowing who my guest was, I'm sure you can find a way to be a little nicer to him."

Now an embarrassed smile appears on Jasmine's face. Obviously she didn't like what Maddalena just revealed. Then she looks at me. Her green eyes are so intense it takes my breath away. And she continues looking at me. For a long time. Too long.

Rewind

Maddalena's hand is raised, immobile. Jasmine is still looking at the spot where I was just a few seconds ago. The girls on the sofas don't move a muscle. The whip of one of the dominatrixes is frozen in an s-shape in the air. I look at the face of the waitress: her expression is a mixture of fear, dread and anticipation. In the back, the girl with the strap-on is frozen in the middle of a thrust.

It's a joke. What else could this be?

I approach the girl nearest to me. There's an expression of pleasure on her face. Her friend is kneeling down at her feet, her head between her legs.

It's a little embarrassing, but I decide to move my fingers towards her. Rather than stopping on her skin, my hand goes through her. She isn't made from matter. I don't know what she is.

I turn and look around me and then down below. My feet are not on the floor, I'm hovering a few centimeters above it. I look up at the ceiling and slowly fly towards it. I get close and reach my hand out to touch it. My fingers disappear inside the material hanging over me.

As I look towards the windows, I start flying towards them. Not even the curtains are real. My hand and then my arm disappear through the wall. Then my head. I close my eyes, instinctively. When I open them up again, I'm flying a few hundred meters over the sea. Maddalena's villa is just a dot in the water.

I look down and start to descend. I think of the waves further down and suddenly find myself above them. They're frozen, too.

I go down even lower. I enter the water. I don't feel anything. I even put my head underwater. I continue breathing.

I come back up to the surface. I stop breathing. I realize I don't need to breathe.

It's a dream.

"No, it's not a dream. It's a system error."

"Who's speaking?" I ask.

"You can give me any form you want."

Jasmine Fantini appears in front of me.

"Why is everything frozen?"

"You could call it a system crash."

"And what exactly crashed?"

"Your universe."

"Mine?"

"Sure, we're inside of it now."

"But there are actually billions of other creatures besides me in this universe."

"No, it's just you living here. It's your projection. You're the one who created it and you're the one who controls it."

"No, I can't believe this. If it was true, how could so many things happen in ways that I don't want them to?"

"You decided to insert a few difficulties and you defined which obstacles you wanted to overcome."

"Me? I'm the one who created the wars, the mafia, injustice, children who die from hunger?"

"Yes, everything is a part of your being."

"And why did I do it?"

"To grow. You created tests to overcome so that you'd come out of this life enriched and improved."

"What's beyond this life?"

"You'll see once you're out."

"Who are you?"

"I'm...you."

"Me?"

"Yes. I'm sorry, I have to reset the level."

"Which level?"

"Unfortunately I made some errors in, well, let's call it the programming, so this level needs to be reset."

"Which errors?"

"Well...remember how you use power-ups in video games? 'God Mode' power-ups make you invincible, and 'Infinite Ammo' give you infinite ammunition. In this case, I accidentally set the level with something similar."

"Why?"

"Programming a universe isn't a game. Sometimes errors happen. Even in superior dimensions there are beta versions of things, it's just the level of complexity that's different."

"But I don't understand, what power-ups are you talking about?"

"You haven't noticed how, every time you face an obstacle, you come out stronger than you went in? The system is trying to maintain a balance based on your initial instructions, but in reality your power has grown too much in too little time. At this rate you would have become a sort of god upon earth and the experience you would gain from this level wouldn't have done you any good."

"The luck! The luck that seemed so incredibly excessive..."

"Bravo! You started playing Doom 4 with Alessio, but it was no longer challenging. You were on the brink of bankruptcy when you got that call from Sabauda Bank. Then you used your patent to conquer half the world with your technology. The system tried to rebalance everything by putting the virus in the payment system, but you created Star Bank. Another attempt at re-equilibrium, with the laundering scandal, but things didn't work and publication of the recordings threw everything off track. Then the interview and the power-up that led to your electoral campaign, naturally won with stunning results. Even at Maddalena Alessi's house, despite the ambiguous reasons why you were there, you had the chance to turn the tables. You and Jasmine would have fallen in love. At this point a re-equilibrium of the system is impossible, so we need to reset the level and start again from the top."

"And when are you going to do that?"

"It's not me who wants to do it, but you. I am you."

"How do you reset it?"

"All you have to do is want to. This is your universe: when you express a desire that's really pure, reality bends to your wishes."

"Really?"

"Sure, it's one of the things you discover while living. You've heard it called many different things: enlightenment, purity, true love."

"And if I decide to go on?"

"You're the one who decided to stop everything. The deepest part of you realized that this flow of events wasn't going to be useful to you and so you pressed the pause key. If you want to go onwards, go right ahead."

The full moon is shining above us. The celestial light makes Jasmine look more beautiful than ever. We're suspended in the void. Under us the black sea is divided into half by the reflection of the heavenly body.

You would have fallen in love. Wow! If I decide to go on, I can go back and everything would resume from where we were. I'd spend the rest of my life with the girl I've always wanted.

I'm reasonably sure that I'm going to have a really great life with these power-ups.

I look directly at her. She's younger, more beautiful and sensual than ever. Her eyes seem to be emitting a light as intense as the stars. But once again, she's unreachable.

"Ok. Let's restart the level."

The Kingdom of Turlis

1

"Antelmo, sweetie, dinner is almost ready. Finish up what you're doing and come to the table! I don't want you playing with your cell phone when I put these hot dishes down!"

Anna is standing over the stove. Her wide, white pants fall softly along her legs. She's wearing a tank top. It's a beautiful summer Saturday evening.

For the umpteenth time, I'm furiously intent on scrutinizing the potential for road access with the navigation system.

If I could only find a way to travel along that path, I'd save myself five miles on every trip.

My wife Anna and I live in a nice little cottage in the foothills. Our home is separated from the house of our neighbor, Costantino Valenti, by a footpath. The short stretch is closed off by a little barrier about thirty centimeters high, beyond which there's a field. The green grass stretches out to the highway, just about a hundred and fifty yards from our houses.

Because of the builder's laziness and problems with municipal regulations, no direct connection to the highway was made. Instead, we need to drive down a little street that loops around for miles, passing dozens of little houses just like our own, plunged into the green forest.

Valenti is elderly. He doesn't leave his house and naturally isn't interested in getting downtown quickly. Anna and I, however, go to work, the movies, restaurants and to see friends. Every time, we have to wind through the hills on our way home.

Neighbors can really be pains in the neck sometimes. Ours is, as a matter of fact.

Enough. This has got to end!

"Darling, I'm going to go check and see if I closed the garage. I think I might have left it open," I tell Anna. I leave quickly, avoiding the incoming complaints.

I take a plank from the toolshed and carry it out under my arm to the walkway. I place one end on top of the little divider and the other end on the ground.

Finally! Let's see if he can stop me now!

I hurry back to the garage, jump onto the seat of my Honda CR 250 and accelerate down the path. The plank has no problem supporting the weight of the motor and, in the blink of an eye, I cross the field and find myself on the highway.

Wow! I got here without having to drive around seven hills!

When I passed Valenti's house, I thought I saw someone pull back the window curtain. *Am I just paranoid? I'm already dreaming about the neighbor at night!*

I don't think Anna is going to be very happy when she finds out about my little excursion. The newsstand is only fifty yards away. I decide to go and buy her the latest issue of Glamour. My kind gesture should mitigate her impending irritation.

I'm thrilled by the idea of going to and from the newsstand without having to drive pointlessly for miles.

A police car is coming towards me down the other lane. *No way!* Maybe they have something else to do, maybe they'll leave me alone.

Not quite! They turn their lights on and stop in the middle of the road, their turn signals blinking. They get ready to do a U-turn and catch up with me. And I'm on a souped-up Honda without a helmet.

Okay, let's pretend that I didn't notice them. I'll just keep going and, once I get to the first side street, I'll turn right. Then I'll reach the forest where I can lose them. I really don't want to get a fine for this little excursion. At any rate, they couldn't have caught my license number, not with all the mud from this morning that's still covering up the plate!

In any case, I decide to not accelerate too much. If they do manage to stop me, I'll at least avoid a fine for speeding.

I've almost reached the end of the perimeter wall around the first cottage. Beyond that it's just forest.

Sirens! Crap! I'm only driving without a helmet! I'm not some kind of criminal!

Game over. I decide to stop. A forty or fifty Euro fine isn't going to ruin me.

The police's Fiat Punto approaches, sirens screaming and lights on.

Something's not right. The cop on the passenger side takes out his gun. It's the first time in my life that I've ever seen a cop take a weapon out of his holster.

The car comes closer. The cop's gun is pointed towards the sky. Then, slowly, he lowers it towards me.

I don't hang around to watch. I hit the gas and escape into the woods.

2

As I drive in between the trees, I realize that my body is racked by shivers. I'm scared and worried.

I had my head uncovered! I'm terrorized, thinking that the cops might have recognized me. *But they didn't get close enough!* And besides, I haven't gotten a fine in ten years, and the city is full of Hondas like mine. I stop to check the plate. It's covered with enough mud, they couldn't have read the letters.

Anna! Dinner!

I stop getting lost in pointless thoughts and concentrate on where I'm going. I know these woods like the back of my hand. I can avoid the highway and other busy roads. I only cross through the woods and fields. I drive very stealthily.

When I'm just 150 yards from my house, I notice something strange.

Valenti! It's him, standing at the front door. *He's talking to the cops!* Their Punto is parked just a little further away, the doors open and the lights still on.

But why are they after me? They could have gotten my Honda mixed up with that of some gypsy wanted for burglary of the cottages in the neighborhood. Maybe Valenti is just complaining about how I illegally crossed the pedestrian footpath on my motorcycle. The police shouldn't care too much about something like that.

One of the two cops looks in my direction. I've stopped at the edge of the woods, hidden by the trees. Maybe they heard the sound of the motor as I came closer. I turn off the motor. The cop turns back to talk with Valenti.

I turn on the motor again and point the motorcycle towards the direction I came from. I slowly navigate through the woods.

If only I could call Anna! Why didn't I take my phone with me?

I drive slowly for a few minutes. This time I have no idea where to go. I think I could go home in a few hours. The cops would have gone to look for gypsies somewhere else. Anna will be furious, but at least this whole ordeal will be over.

One, two, three, four police sirens! And above me, the sound of a helicopter propeller. This is unreal! What's going on?

If they're looking for me with a helicopter, it won't be hard to detect the movement of the motorcycle through the leaves of the trees. *I need to figure out how to get out of here, quickly! If I surrender, what do I risk? At the most a fine for driving a two-wheeler without a helmet and with the license plate covered up.* At this point, the best thing to do would be to end this whole ordeal.

I head towards the sound of the police sirens. I'm almost in the open when something inside of me tells me no. In my mind, I see the gun pointed in my direction. I can't go forward.

When people are overcome with panic, they often do stupid things. I know what I'm about to do is one of those stupid things. I turn off the motorcycle, lay it on the ground, cover it with leaves and continue on foot.

After a few minutes I reach a cottage deep in the woods. I decide to ask for help. I'm not a criminal, but a respected professional. I can say that I twisted my ankle while walking through the woods and need help. I'll stay in the house just until the helicopter and the police cars go on to continue their search elsewhere.

I ring the bell.

No answer.

Again.

I don't hear anything.

One last time.

Nothing.

I'm about to go when I hear the sound of the helicopter propellers. They seem to be heading straight towards me. I decide to ring one last time, but I notice that the gate has been left ajar. Maybe they didn't hear the bell inside.

"Anybody home?" I ask in a voice that's not too loud.

The helicopter seems to be coming even closer.

I walk through the gate. As I come towards the house, I continue to announce my presence:

"Excuse me, I need some help."

I enter.

"I'm sorry to disturb you. I was in the woods and I hurt my foot. I need medical attention."

Everything is quiet in the house.

"Hello, excuse me, this isn't a burglary! I have a little problem. Is there anybody who could help me?"

The noise of the helicopter is louder now. The door behind me is still open. I decide to close it, so that the helicopter doesn't notice anything strange.

Just in time! The noise of the helicopter now seems to be coming from directly above the cottage.

I move away from the door and enter what looks like the living room. It's a little outdated. The furniture is made from a dark, cheap wood. The living room has windows on two sides, the third side flanks the open kitchen, and there's a large piece of furniture on the fourth side that serves as both a pantry and a bookcase. Further along there's an enormous grandfather clock, right in front of the windows.

I go towards the clock, move a curtain back just a few inches and watch where the helicopter's going. It seems to be moving away. *Finally!*

Now, think! It doesn't seem like anybody's here. The owners must have forgotten to close the door when they left. The best thing to do would be to stay here for a few minutes to be sure that the helicopter and the police are far away. Then I'll leave. Now that the danger seems to be moving away, I'd prefer to avoid running into the owners of the house when they come back. An attorney like me doesn't really need to be accused of trespassing in someone's home.

Dinner! Anna will be beside herself with rage. If only I hadn't forgotten my cell phone!

Click, clack. I hear the front door open. I hide behind the huge clock.

"Don't hide yourself in regret
Just love yourself and you're set
I'm on the right track, baby
I was born this way, born this way."

It's a beautiful female voice singing. She must be carrying a lot of bags, because it takes her a few trips to carry everything into the house before she pushes the door shut with her shoulder.

Then she enters the living room and, lucky for me, heads towards the kitchen. I peek out just a bit from the corner of the clock to see who I'm dealing with.

It's a girl, brunette, not very tall. She's wearing purple sweats, Converse sneakers and a greenish tank top. She seems a little heavy-set. She's got freckles. She has an iPod in a little holster wrapped around her arm. She still has the earbuds in her ears. She's carrying a few shopping bags in her hand.

49

"Don't be a drag, just be a queen
Don't be a drag, just be a queen
Don't be a drag, just be a queen
Don't be..."

Ok, if she has her headphones in, she won't hear me as I try to leave. When my wife Anna brings things home, she always starts putting what she bought into the fridge, the freezer and the pantry. This girl also places the bags on the kitchen table and starts to do the same. The problem is that she's very quick. She puts her hands in the bag, turns towards the pantry and immediately turns back again to take something else.

Finally she stops to look for something in the fridge. It seems like the right moment to me. I'm about to leave my hiding place when she turns around again.

I brace myself, my shoulders against the wall. When I peeked out I thought she looked towards me, but then she took something else from the bag and continued doing what she had been doing.

She couldn't have seen me!

"No matter gay, straight or bi
Lesbian, transgendered life
I'm on the right track, baby
I was born to survive"

I try to figure out what to do. If she sees me, she'll probably be scared, and I have no idea how to handle that kind of situation. I could wait for her to finish putting everything away in the pantry. When she goes to her room to change, I can leave the house without her noticing.

I look at the windows. They seem like the kind of windows that make a lot of noise when you open them. The only way to leave is the way I came in.

DONG DONG DONG. The chiming of the clock cuts through my nervousness, making me jump. My hand heavily hits the side of the huge clock. The woman stops singing.

She must have heard me, despite the music in her ears. I made too much noise!

I remain frozen in my position, holding my breath.

Her steps cautious, the girl seems to be moving away from the living room.

If she calls the police, I'm screwed! I think the best thing to do is

50

to stop waiting and just escape. If she notices me, I'm a man and I'm surely faster and stronger than her.

A woman wouldn't want to stop me or try to follow me. When they investigate, they'll probably start looking for a little burglary ring.

In any case, if she still hasn't seen me, it's better that she doesn't see me now, so I tiptoe out of my hiding place behind the clock, trying to make as little noise as possible. I run in front of the bookcase. I stop where the living room opens into the foyer. I peek out just to have a look.

She's standing there, frozen, in the center of the foyer, staring right at me.

3

"Were you looking for something?" she asks me.

She must be afraid: I'm taller and surely much stronger than she is. Yet she's standing just a few yards away from me, with her arms down along her sides. She seems calm, even determined. *Maybe she teaches some kind of martial arts.*

"Look, I'm really sorry. I rang your bell looking for help. Then I saw the gate was open so I came in to see if anyone was home. You came in after me, and at that point I was afraid that if you saw me you'd get scared. So I hid, thinking I'd wait until you left the living room. I just wanted to leave the house without bothering you. Again, I'm really sorry. Anyway it's nice to meet you, I'm Attorney Antelmo Ubaldini."

As I speak, she doesn't move a muscle.

Yes, she's got to be some sort of trainer, and she's probably thinking about how she's going to knock me out.

"I know who you are, I've known you for years."

A client? Or a client of another lawyer that I've gone up against in court?

"Ah, okay, I'm really sorry for what happened, but I'm happy we know each other. I was afraid I'd scare you. So I'd say that maybe it's best that I leave you be, given the problem that I've already caused here."

"That's not what I had in mind! You think you can just come into other people's houses and then leave as if nothing happened? You know, as I was coming back home, I noticed a police helicopter patrolling the area. I also passed by a couple cop cars."

"Really? I didn't notice any of that confusion."

She narrows her eyes, unsure, and asks: "So why are you here?"

"I was collecting mushrooms in the woods. Then I twisted my ankle and I decided to look for help. Your place was the first cottage I came to."

"And the mushrooms? Where did you leave them?"

"I had a hard time supporting my own weight, I didn't want to carry the mushrooms, too."

"But now it doesn't look like you have too many trouble staying on your feet." She looks at me, probing.

"In fact, my ankle still hurts really bad, but I don't think this is the right moment to ask you for anything to help with it."

"But no! Of course! Come on, make yourself comfortable on the sofa and let me see what I can do."

Her tone is now gentle, but her words seem strangely threatening. She seems a little too friendly.

She moves towards me, passes me by and goes towards the pantry.

"Don't stand there like a stick, get on the couch and take off your shoe and sock. I'll look for something to help with the pain and a bandage."

"That's very kind of you Miss, and I don't want to take advantage but, if you really want to help me, could you let me make a call first? I left a little while ago and since I haven't come back yet, my wife is probably worried about me."

"Sorry, no can do. Unfortunately I don't have a landline and the cell doesn't get any reception here, Antelmo."

So how does she communicate with the rest of the world when she's home? For a girl with an iPod attached to her arm, she's not that hi-tech.

"And please, don't call me Miss. My name's Irene."

"Ah, okay. Listen, Irene, I'm going to sound really rude here but I don't really remember when we met. Can you refresh my memory?"

"Oh, you would never guess how long it's been. And look, here you are! Now let's get this little problem out of the way."

Irene comes towards me holding a pair of scissors, a spray can, a tube of cream and a glass with an effervescent tablet dissolving in water. She sits down on the table in front of the sofa.

"So let me see this banged-up ankle. In the meantime drink this, it'll make the pain go away."

A little embarrassed, I bring my nude foot up to this girl who I can't remember for the life of me. She takes it and puts it in her lap.

"Does it hurt here?" she asks me.

I try to remember where the pain is located when you twist your ankle. I had some actual injuries a few times when I played soccer.

"No, it's a little higher up. Right there!" I answer.

"Drink up, come on. Or do you just want to lie there and suffer?" Irene asks me.

I look at the medicine. The water is tinged with purple. Usually I don't like taking medicine, but I don't want to offend her. I down the entire glass in four swallows. In the meantime, she starts spraying my perfectly healthy ankle.

"All done! How do you feel?" she asks, putting my foot back on the floor.

"Thanks, Irene. The pain seems to be going away."

Without responding, she gets up and puts everything back in the kitchen. I get up too. Or, better said, I try to get up. My foot remains frozen on the ground. I try to move. It feels like it's glued. *What kind of medicine did she use?* I try to pull my leg up with my hands.

"Don't waste your energy. You won't be able to move it," Irene says.

She's sitting on the kitchen table. She's holding a glass of wine in her hand. She looks at me and sighs. "Oh, sweetie," she continues. "Look at how scared your little eyes are! You can't move your little foot anymore? Wait for me to help you. *Eina ta sturam!*"

My foot, ankle and calf slowly start to shine with the same color as the effervescent medicine. I rub my eyes, thinking I'm hallucinating.

"What the...?"

"Don't worry, it's a little trick for apprentices," Irene tells me. She places the glass of wine on the table and comes towards me. "But it works, doesn't it?" she asks me, caressing my cheek. "Don't tell me that you've never seen anything like it? Cloradil must be very good at hiding things."

"Cloradil?"

"You don't even know her real name? What do you call her, then, that adorable little creature who makes your little dinners?"

"Anna? Are you talking about my wife?"

"Your wife? Do you really think she's your wife?"

I don't know how she was able to freeze my leg, but this woman is definitely mentally insane.

"You still don't understand? Magic, spells...you think it's all made up, don't you? *Al fami spes eriat.*"

My foot begins to slowly rise through the air. When it's up to my waist, I lose my balance and fall over the back of the sofa. But the foot doesn't stop rising upwards. It pulls me along with it. My back rises off of the cushions. When my foot manages to touch the ceiling, I find myself hanging with my head down, firmly anchored.

"You find it easier to believe me now?" Irene asks me, just a few inches away from my head.

I think about Anna. Why did I walk into this house? I don't know who this woman is, and I really want to be home with my wife, eating one of her delicious weekend dinners.

"Listen, Irene, I think I made a mistake coming into your house. Please forgive me. Now, though, I want to leave and go home to my wife."

"Oh, little Antelmo, did I scare you? You're right, I'm the one who should be asking you to forgive me, I was very rude. Go home. Your family is the most important thing. Go right ahead. *Is medil ancorat.*"

I'm back on the floor, standing. I try to move my foot. This time it lifts without any problems. I have a thousand questions, but something tells me that if Irene is willing to let me go now, it's better that I hurry up and get out of here as soon as I can.

"Ok, goodbye."

I go to shake her hand. She doesn't move. I turn around and head towards the front, place my hand on the doorknob and open the door to thick, thick fog.

The woods and the trees have disappeared. I kneel down on the threshold. I feel out in front of me, where the little front path must be. My hands grope about in the void. I lean out further. I try to reach my hand underneath the house floor: nothing.

"If I were you, I'd be careful not to fall," Irene advises me.

A frigid breeze cuts through the fog. I feel like I'm freezing. I close the door.

"We're not in your forest anymore, dear Antelmo."

"So where are we?" I ask.

"I'm sure you'd rather not know."

"Irene, who are you, really?"

"I'm the best friend of Cloradil, your wife. You know, we really love each other. We were so close!"

The sarcasm in her voice is palpable.

"And what do you want from me?"

"From you? Let's say there are a couple things we need to work out."

"Where are we?"

"We're headed home."

"Home?"

"Yep. The Kingdom of Turlis."

"Where's that?"

"It's not very close to Earth. But I have to go now. See you later."

I'm dreaming, I must be dreaming. Irene heads towards the door, opens it, takes a step out and disappears into the void.

I follow her to the door, but there's no trace of her in the fog. I hurry to close the door so that the icy air doesn't freeze me.

I'm alone.

4

Alone. In a house flying through the thick fog. I still can't believe it. I pull the curtains away from the window to look outside. Fog. *No, I don't think we're anywhere near the woods around my house.* Cloradil, my wife, what does she have to do with magic? No, none of this makes any sense.

I was hanging upside-down with my foot glued to the ceiling. And half of my leg was glowing! How does a human limb glow from inside?

There must some sort of logical explanation for all of this. Maybe I can find it in this house.

I head towards the kitchen. I look through the fridge and pantry. Nothing out of the ordinary. The only place left to explore is upstairs.

A queen-sized bed, a bathroom and a little room for kids with a bunk bed. It's all decorated in the same style. This house seems old. It's not the type of furniture you normally see in a cottage in a residential area where real estate costs two thousand Euro per square foot.

I look through the dresser and the closet in the master bedroom. The clothes stored here are flimsy, and at least twenty years old.

If Irene was really a witch, wouldn't she at least make herself a more fashionable wardrobe?

And what if this house wasn't hers?

Where am I going? And why?

The questions continue to spin through my mind.

"Alia fas no sdreil imas catel biron."

Oh my god, I know that voice: it's Anna, my wife.

"You can still do it. There's no time for explanations, but you can still save yourself. You need to have faith. Open the window and jump out. Don't be afraid, I'll save you."

The voice seems to be coming from the fog. I rush to open the window, which lets out an unpleasant squeak.

The freezing air immediately gives me goose bumps. Outside of the house, in the fog, the temperature seems to be plunging dozens of degrees below zero. I turn towards the bed, take a sheet and wrap it around my body. Even now I feel like I'm freezing.

I turn back to the window. I hang outside of it. Where is her voice coming from?

"Don't wait. There's no time to spare, you can't go back anymore," my wife's voice continues.

"Anna, where are you? Why can't I see you?"

"Antelmo, don't dilly-dally. You'll be lost forever in just a few seconds. I won't be able to do anything for you. Climb out the window. Come back to me. I need you."

"Anna, please, answer me. Where are you?"

"Do it now. You're almost out of time."

I lift my right leg over the windowsill. I try to see if I can make anything out beyond the window, but it's all fog. And cold.

Holding on to the sill, I lift my left leg. I'm terrorized by the idea of falling into the void.

"Stop!"

It's Irene's voice. Her figure appears in the doorway of the bedroom.

"There's nothing outside there. If you do, you die."

I feel entirely hopeless. I'm terrorized by the idea of letting myself fall into the void, but I can't stay in this house any longer.

"Come here, Antelmo. There's no sense in sacrificing your life. You've already given too much to Cloradil," Irene says.

"Antelmo, my love, there's no time left. Do it for me. Do it for us. Come back to your wife. I'm here, waiting for you."

Again, it's my wife's voice, it's Anna. All I want is to be back in her arms. She's right. I've always trusted her.

In the meantime, Irene has moved closer to me.

I lift my left leg over the sill. I'm outside of the window. I hang onto the outer edge of the sill for just a moment and then let myself go.

A tight grip grasps me and starts to lift me. With my head just barely beyond the sill, I notice that it's Irene's hand. *But how can she be so strong?*

She pulls me up inside the window and I let her. I want to resist but I'm still not completely convinced that jumping into the void was the right thing to do. I'm afraid.

"Antelmo, my love..."

Anna's voice is even further away.

"That's an echo-voice," Irene seems to be reading my mind. "She launched it with the mistrofal of the Earth once she understood

58

where we were headed. That's why she didn't answer you. Those were just words chasing after you. She couldn't hear you. And if you fell into the void, you would simply have died."

Rage rises up inside of me.

"I don't believe you! I don't know who or what you are, but that was my wife! Why are you doing this to me? How could you have kidnapped me and made me prisoner in this house?"

"You were the one who entered this house out of your own free will. It was your choice. Perhaps Turlis came into your heart and showed you the right way."

While she talks, I hear the last echo of Anna's voice.

"Antelmooo..."

With a sudden twitch I lunge towards the window and leap outside. Just before my body is completely outside of the house, a very strong flash blinds me and forces me to close my eyelids. I feel my face hit the wet ground.

I open my eyes. The house is still in front of me, but now it is pure white and splendid. The walls are made of white marble. Inside the bedroom, the closet, dresser and bed are now encrusted and embellished with gems.

Irene is covered in white veils. Her hair is pulled back into a braid that wraps around her head, like a crown.

I look around. I'm on a small lawn, sprinkled with flowers of every color and type. Just a little further from me there's a bubbling brook, beyond which the forest begins. I see lots of little hills in the distance. There are many other gleaming little houses. The sky is astoundingly bright.

Something attracts my curiosity in the soft shadow of a house near me. The sun is shining right at me. There shouldn't be a shadow pointing towards the star. I turn around. Behind me I see three other suns, one similar to the first, the other two much smaller.

I have no idea where I am. But this is definitely not Earth.

5

"We need to get moving. Unfortunately we couldn't land closer to the Palace. We still have a little ways to go here. Enondil should be here any minute."

I'm still on the ground, admiring the enchanting landscape that spreads out before my eyes.

Irene talks to me from inside the bedroom. I think she's doing something in the closet, which is shining with a thousand colors of light.

"What is this house, Irene?"

"It's my house. You knew that, right?"

"Yes, sure, but usually women's houses don't serve as means of transport between a forest and another planet."

"In fact it took a lot of time to prepare this transport. We've spent decades scanning thousands of planets looking for you and, once we found you, the operation took years to prepare."

"The operation? What kind of...?"

"Here's Enondil. Come on, let's go, we don't have a moment to waste."

I turn around and see a man inside of a gigantic bubble coming towards me, full speed ahead. The man is comfortably lying on a couch created from the same material as the bubble and suspended in the middle of it. When he's just a few yards away, I recognize him and instinctively get up to run and hide.

"No, no Antelmo, don't run away. It's Enondil. He'll come with us."

"Enondil? It's the policeman who wanted to shoot me!" I protest, rather exasperated.

Enondil jumps down from the bubble and heads towards me.

"He still doesn't remember anything?" he asks, turning towards Irene.

"No, nothing. Less than nothing. Cloradil knew what she was doing," Irene answers.

"Cloradil, you mean Anna, my wife. Where is she? Is she coming with us too? When can I see her?"

Irene and Enondil exchange a knowing smile.

Enondil says: "Let's leave now, or we could be too late. Come on," he continues, turning towards me.

We enter the strange bubble. Our bodies pass through the walls, as if they were only made of light. The sofa, on the other hand, is elastic and bears our weight. The bubble rises into the sky.

"What is this...vehicle? How did you build it?" I ask.

Irene smiles: "We didn't build it. We manifested it."

"Another illusion?" I ask, not very convinced.

"*Ois midal musri gan,*" Enondil recites.

The bubble becomes a pyramid and the walls take on a light blue glow.

"The bubble is better, a little more aerodynamic, but the pyramid will work," Irene explains.

An immense noise rips through the air. We instinctively bring our hands up to our ears and look towards where the deafening noise is coming from.

"It's her. Bring Antelmo to safety. I'm going to..." Irene says.

I don't hear the end of her sentence. A beam of dim light, from a point in the sky above us, shines towards us and pushes me down.

Falling from this height, impact with the ground will surely kill me. It's over. Instead I find myself in the water of the bubbling brook I saw in front of Irene's house.

The beam disappears. I try to go up to the surface. A powerful force magnetizes me downwards. I look down to find out what it is. I see that a luminous surface has opened between two rocks. It seems as if the magnetizing force is coming from there.

When I'm almost near the light, I try to resist. I brace my knees and elbows against the rocks.

"Come on, come home. You can't keep the portal open much longer. It's me, Anna, your wife. Look for yourself: this is our home."

It's like a TV screen: inside the light I see the image of Anna. She's standing in our living room. I even see my smartphone on the table. She's wearing the same clothes she had on when I left. Near the kitchen, the table is set with the pasta already on the plates.

I still don't understand what kind of strange nightmare I've gotten into, but what I see in front of my eyes is truly my home. It's over. But this time I'm asking Anna for explanations.

"Come on, now! Careful, they're coming!"

I jump feet-first into the light source while I look to see who's following me. Irene, right behind me, is swimming with a rock in her hand. I try to take shelter and see out of the corner of my eye that Enondil has almost caught up with me. The rock bashes heavily into my head. Two hands grab my wrists. I pass out.

6

"If she was able to send out a space-time signal, she must have grown much more stronger than we had thought."

"Impossible! Ibril never let her out of his sight! She couldn't have absorbed all that power in just thirty-three years."

Enondil and Irene seem rather excited.

I open my eyes. I'm lying face-down on the transparent sofa. The landscape flies by underneath me.

"What powers? Who is Ibril?" I stammer.

A few seconds of silence pass. I imagine they're exchanging their usual knowing look. I sit up. I look at their faces, first his, then hers.

"Tell me!" The commanding tone of my voice seems to rattle them.

"Ibril is Costantino Valenti," Irene says in a low voice, as if apologizing.

"Valenti, the nosy neighbor? Are you joking? What does that obnoxious old man have to do with all of this?"

"How dare you call him that! He's been so faithful to you!" Enodil starts, enraged.

"Enough!" Irene interrupts. "Everything in due time."

"No," I say. "I want to know everything, right now!"

"When we found you, some of us had already been transferred to Earth to find out what Cloradil's plans were and to prepare for your removal. Enondil and Ibril were among these people."

"Why? Who are you? What do you want from me?" I ask again, exasperated.

"Antelmo, you already have the answers to your own questions," Irene tells me gently, "but you still refuse to recognize this inside you. You have to accept all of this within yourself first, otherwise there's no explanation that could possibly manage to convince you."

"Deep down inside I can't find any answers."

"That's what we were afraid of. Cloradil picked a primitive planet like the Earth just so you wouldn't make any contacts."

"Primitive? Earth isn't primitive at all!"

"Antelmo," Irene's tone is almost maternal, "how much time do Earthlings spend on issues that have nothing to do with eating, sex, arguing, war and vanity?"

"What does that have to do with anything? Sure, maybe a lot of people only care about those kinds of things, but we also have scientists, philosophers, doctors and a lot of people who do good on Earth. And..."

"Yes," Irene interrupts, "but do you let these people guide you or govern you? Or do you willingly follow whoever puts out smiling advertisements, beautiful little faces and tempting promises? Evolved planets are guided by love of knowledge, research and spiritual growth. Cloradil chose Earth because it's about as far as you can get from the Kingdom of Turlis!"

"Chose? When?"

Enondil and Irene exchange glances, then lower their eyes. They remain silent, their faces lost in some painful memory.

We're flying over a house surrounded by fountains and waterways that spill into a little lake. In the middle, there's an island with dozens of kids standing around a woman.

"That's a school. And she is a magic teacher. You can recognize her from the braid circling her head, like a crown," Irene explains, turning off the motor of the pyramid.

"Like..." I start to ask.

"Yes, like mine!"

"So, you teach magic?"

"Not just magic."

"Magic," I repeat, absorbed in my own thoughts. I look down. One boy is standing up. He brings both of his hands in front of him and turns his palms towards one another. A point of orange light starts to take shape between his hands, growing larger every second.

"It's a memory sphere. He can put his memories inside, as well as his feelings and fears," Irene explains.

There seem to be images in the sphere. From this high up, I can't really make them out.

"Magic is the principal method to examine the laws of the universe and the laws of the soul," Irene articulates her words carefully, as if it was especially important that I understand what she's telling me.

"Magic for what's inside and outside of us," my words seem to be evoking distant memories.

"Exactly!"

"There are a lot of ancient texts that deal with magic on Earth. Every once in a while there's an interesting movie on TV or in the

64

theaters on wizards. But I never believed in all of that."

"Why not?" Irene asks.

"Because I always thought it was a load of crap! And Anna always agreed with me. I can't imagine what she has to do with all of this."

"When did you two meet?"

"We went to the same kindergarten and have stayed together ever since."

"And what was she like?"

I smile. Anna's personality is a little difficult to explain.

"Anna is a little bossy. She has the personality of a leader and likes to do things her own way."

"So she always had a certain level of influence over you?"

"She was the stronger of us two. Between a man and a woman, there's always one who's in charge. It's usually the woman. But she always gave me my own space."

"Your space for what?"

"Tennis games, Friday nights with my friends, games at the stadium on Sundays."

"And you two never had any arguments?"

"We always talked about everything. It's normal, when you're together!"

"But who decided what you did, where you went, what you watched on TV?"

"I'd say...maybe...she did a little more often. But she always listened to me and considered my point of view."

"Did she ever tell you her opinions on your career or other important choices in life?"

"Yes, of course. But a lot of the time I was the one asking for her advice!"

"Why did you think you couldn't make those choices alone?"

"No, that's not it at all. It's normal to confide in the people around you."

"Was she the only person who told you what to do, or were there others?"

"She was my girlfriend for a long time and then became my wife. It's only natural that she'd be the most important person in my life."

"Did she think the same thing?"

"Of course!"

65

I don't want to admit it, but Anna had always been very authoritarian. In fact, she had been a real dictator with me since we were little. We never did anything that she didn't want to do. Every once in a while I would complain and get angry, but everything would work out in the end.

7

The pyramid starts flying again.

"Here we are. We'll start to see it," Enondil announces.

My eyes look towards where he's pointing. The outline of an impressive building stands out against the horizon. We slowly come closer and the contours appear more clearly. My jaw drops.

It's not just a *palace*. It's a fairy-tale construction, which seems to defy every law of physics. It's several stories tall, floating in the air, surrounded by infinite islands connected by rainbow bridges. On each island there are buildings, some of which have solid walls, others which seem to be made of pure energy.

Trees, flowers, lawns and ponds are everywhere, inside and outside of the houses. The water courses form stupendous waterfalls that go from one island to the other. I've never seen anything so marvelous.

Enondil and Irene are staring at me. I don't understand why they're scrutinizing me so closely. *Are they hoping that this place will remind me of something?*

"It's too dangerous. We can't bring him to the Well when he's like this," Enondil, visibly worried, tells Irene.

"There's no other choice. Even I hoped something would reawaken in him. But if it hasn't happened, then the Well is the only place that can help," she replies.

"But she'll see him in the Well and try to contact him!"

"Not necessarily. Maybe she'll be looking somewhere else at that moment. Anyway, I have faith in him."

"Sorry for the interruption, but what's the Well? And who's going to see me? Anna? My wife?"

They look at each other, exasperated. Maybe they don't like the fact that I keep calling her *my wife*. Maybe they thought they could mess up my mind with all of their babble, but I know who I am.

They didn't need to tell me when we were near the Well. On an island right in the middle of the palace, higher than all the others, there's a hole about twenty yards in diameter that creates a beam of soft light, which descends thousands of feet into the ground below.

"It goes down to the middle of the planet. Down there, you can connect to many other worlds through other dimensions," Irene explains.

"Through other dimensions?" I ask.

"Yes, a lot of energy is transmitted through dimensions. But even physical bodies can travel through dimensions, even though it's extremely onerous. To go to the Earth from here, for example, we had to cross through another dimension."

"The   fog?"

"Exactly. We weren't in a physical universe."

"But...?"

"Wait. I'm afraid we don't have any time left. You need to go into the   Well."

"Me? Where?"

The pyramid lands on the island. There are dozens of people doing something on little wells of light that are floating in the air.

"What are they?"

"Those are mistrofals. They are powerful magnifiers of magical energy. A powerful wizard with one of these can bridge infinite distances. Cloradil used them to fling a space-time arrow on this world and open a breach between here and the Earth, which you could have passed through."

"Why doesn't she come here, if she doesn't want to lose me so much?"

"Because she's not powerful enough yet."

"And how do you get more power?"

Enondil interrupts, saying to Irene: "You're right, all we can do is go to the Well."

They seem defeated. I feel like I let them down, but I have no idea what they want from me.

"We can't help you anymore. But you can try to help yourself," Irene tells me.

"Here, where?" I ask. "What should I do?"

"Enter."

"I have to jump into that thing? No way!"

Irene comes in front of me and places her hand on my shoulder. Again, her green eyes look into my own.

"You'll find yourself in this well. And, probably, she'll be there as well. You can choose. Decide what you want to be for yourself."

She's almost convincing.

"What should I do?"

"Nothing in particular. Just take a step forward and let yourself

68

go. There are only memories in there."

"Memories of what?"

"Of this and your other lives."

"Other lives?"

"Yes, the life in which..."

"Irene!" Enondil interrupts. "It's up to him." Then he turns to me: "Go. If you want to go back to your life on Earth, you'll have the option down there. And it'll probably be the person you call your *wife* who gives you that option."

There we go, that's a convincing motivation. I take a step forward and let myself fall down the Well.

The last words I manage to hear Irene say are "Let the connections guide you."

8

I'm floating in the darkness of the Well.

A distant glow seems to gradually grow stronger. It's coming closer.

It's light, suspended in nothing. Slowly, a few images become more clear.

I see myself, hiding in the storage closet of my parents' house. We're playing a game called *the dark room*. A little light shines through the keyhole of the door in front of me. I bend down and put my eye against the little hole. My mother's walking down the hallway, bringing the pizzas to the table. She doesn't know that I'm hiding in the storage closet.

I've always loved this game, which usually ends with me suddenly opening the door to frighten my mother.

Why am I seeing this scene from my life? Is this one of the connections Irene was talking about?

Another light approaches and comes up next to the first.

I see a man sitting on a throne, with a crown on his head and a scepter in his hand. A woman stands before him, talking to him. The room lights are dimmed. A splendid stellar map stretches out over their heads.

The woman explains to him, indicating a point on the map above her: "These are the Misos and Mauteris stars. The forms of life living on their planets just discovered the secret to interstellar travel. We should do further research on their level of magic."

It's Irene who's speaking. She looks exactly like she did today.

"Alright, Alissalia. It's a good idea to focus in on this quadrant, where the level of magic is still very low. Considering what level their power has grown to, we can give them new opportunities."

Alissalia? Irene must have another name here.

With one gesture from the king, the planetarium disappears and an intense light shines into the room. I can see the splendid islands of the palace outside of the windows. So the memory of the scene from this second light evidently comes from a place very close to where I am now.

Remember! Irene – Alissalia – had said that I would find

memories of this and other lives.

Connections! Did the darkness also lead me to this scene? *If it's one of my memories, where am I?*

A third light bobs towards me. The scene is intermittent, it disappears and reappears.

The same king as before is on the ground. A luminous green prism is plunged into his heart. A woman is sitting astride him.

"Why did you do it?" the king asks her, speaking with great difficulty.

"Because I want us to stay together. And I want to have the powers that only a queen can have. I'm tired of waiting! How could you not have realized that for all this time?"

"I know you wanted it," the king's voice is weak, "but I couldn't give it to you precisely because you wanted it." His words seem to fade away. "Cloradil, what did you gain from this murder? I'll reincarnate. The wizards will find me, they'll educate me and they'll bring me back to my throne."

Darkness. The memory light fades away.

"How can you be so sure? They may not find you."

The king's face twists into a mask of pain.

"What did you do? Did you use...?"

"Yes. I set the course so that your frequency will reincarnate in a form chosen by me. It's a primitive and violent place, where magic has been forgotten for thousands of years. And I will be there with you. Before anyone can find you, I'll have absorbed most of your powers. You won't be able to recover the knowledge of who you were. I, however, will follow the course that I prepared myself. I'll wake up and I'll regain my powers. And then I'll start to absorb yours. It'll take years, but I'll have all the time I need. And I'll also have the mistrofal, that I've already sent to myself on that planet."

A veil of deep sadness falls over the king's eyes.

"Oh, don't be sad. We'll reincarnate and spend a splendid life together. I'll be a marvelous little wife in our next life. Doesn't that make you feel a little bit better, my love?"

A door on the side of the room opens.

"Your majesty!"

It's the voice of Alissalia, who immediately races towards the king and his assassin.

"Cloradil, what did you do?" Alissalia asks, raising her hands as she runs. A blue ball starts to form.

Cloradil brusquely tears the prism from the king's heart and plunges it into her own chest. Her body falls next to the king's body.

He closes his eyes. The image disappears.

After a few seconds, the king reopens his eyes. The image is faint and very dark. Alissalia is kneeling next to the dying king, and has taken his head into her lap.

Darkness again.

The image reappears one more time, so faint that it can barely be distinguished from all of the surrounding darkness.

The king's eyelids strain to open once more. A tear rolls down Alissalia's face and falls on her cheek.

"Your majesty, I'll find you again and teach you."

Darkness.

Memories! Connections! A king! Cloradil!

How could these memories be mine? What does all of this have to do with me? Who is this king? And why did a woman, who has the name everyone uses to refer to my wife, kill him?

A primitive and violent world. No, that couldn't be Earth. Maybe there's a lot of war and tension, but we're not savages. We study. We grow. We build. We do our best to evolve. And besides, could there possibly exist a place in the universe that's truly pure?

The three lights in front of me disappear. I'm again plunged into deep darkness. From a point further away than the others, a faint light slowly heads towards me. For several long moments, it's barely visible. Then it becomes more intense, brighter, pure.

A newborn is in a cradle created from a luminous material, similar to that of soap bubbles.

A light blue foam surrounds its body, leaving its neck and little head uncovered.

A woman bends down to look at it tenderly. Her blonde hair falls down to her shoulders.

Marvelous sparkling stones, placed a few millimeters away from one another, form the shape of a crown on his head.

The woman sings a sweet melody to the baby.

"Eina sto fil,
ardas mael,
bis or manil
ei tam lual.

Ardin faras
al bel tomir
ei to bras
ol tur momir"

The baby responds with joyful coos. He waves his hands to the rhythm.

"Your majesty, it's a stupendous baby. And he'll be a great king."

Costantino Valenti is speaking. He's wearing a blue tunic and standing behind the queen.

What is my neighbor doing in this memory?

"Dearest Tainador, he'll be a great king if you help us raise him."

"Your Majesty, if he wishes and is worthy, he'll have access to all of the knowledge of our king. Have you already decided on his name?"

"Yes. His name shall be Turlis."

Turlis? The Kingdom of Turlis? Is this baby the future king? Do they want me to believe that I...? No, there's no way. This is all an illusion!

"Antelmo, you're in the Well, right?"

The image in front of me disappears. Anna's voice cuts through the darkness.

"Anna, it's completely dark here. Where are you?"

"Wait, I'll open a portal."

The darkness is broken by a luminous disk similar to the one that was drawing me down to the bottom of the stream, near Irene's house.

"Anna, my darling, how did you find me?"

"It doesn't matter, Antelmo. Now you can come back to me. I don't have the strength to bring you to me if you're in the well. You have to come and meet me."

My wife is in the living room. She's holding the mistrofal in her hands.

73

"Anna, I've seen some...strange things in this place. There was a king who was killed by a woman. And she had the name that people use here for you. In another memory, I was inside the storage closet in my house. That memory is mine. But the others...I don't know what they were about."

"Don't worry, Antelmo, come here. You'll be safe here and I'll explain everything to you."

"Anna, tell me something: what do you know about magic? What do you know about this king? I don't understand, why didn't you tell me anything?"

"Antelmo, I wanted to protect you. I didn't want you to worry. There are worlds out there inhabited by wicked forces. Some of us have the task of protecting others, but it's not always possible to explain what we do."

"You don't think I'm worthy of knowing all this?"

"I'm sorry, Antelmo. Of course you're worthy. I'll tell you about it as soon as I can."

"But we're over thirty years old! And we've known each other since we were six. When did you intend on telling me that you have an instrument for communicating with the rest of the universe?"

"You have every right to be angry. I'll tell you everything, I promise, but there's no time to waste now. Come here before they come back to stop you."

"Okay, darling. I'm sorry. I'm coming. What do I need to do?"

"Go towards the portal you see in front of you. Then go inside of it and you'll be here, next to me. All of this will just seem like a bad memory."

"Okay, but you have to help me, I don't have the courage. Please, come towards the portal. Hold out your hand, otherwise I don't know if I'll be able to."

"Of course, sweetie. Wait."

Anna comes near the portal. She holds out her left hand towards the portal and, with her right hand, keeps her hold on the mistrofal.

"Can I come in? Listen, you need to tell your husband to never again put a plank in our walkway. Do you know that he ruined all of the grass with his motorcycle? Is that how a well-behaved young man acts?"

Costantino Valenti appears at the French doors of our living room with a cane in his hand. Anna turns around, surprised. She obviously wasn't expecting this interruption.

While she's distracted, I place my hands around the portal and pull the mistrofal away from her. She turns immediately towards me.

"Darling, sweetie, what did you do?" she asks.

There's a fear that I've never seen, in so many years together, in her eyes.

"Anna, that old man is Tainador. He came here to take the mistrofal from you."

Costantino starts laughing. "If I wanted to take the mistrofal from her, I had plenty of chances to do it before today."

"It doesn't matter, Mr. Valenti, you don't belong to our world. Go into the portal, go back to your kingdom and leave us alone forever. Otherwise we'll have to throw you in there," I tell him, dryly.

Valenti heads towards the portal. He uses his cane to support his every step. He's a little less in shape than the man I saw in my vision, but other than that, he looks pretty much the same.

"Goodbye, Cloradil." he says, turning to my wife, before going into the portal.

"Very good, my darling," Anna says. "You did the right thing. I couldn't stand him either! And I never would have thought that he was one of our enemies, too. Now that we're finally safe, come on."

Both of us remain silent for a few seconds.

"Goodbye, Anna," I tell her. She looks at me, expressionless. "You expected to find a primitive and savage world on Earth but, in reality, it's a world that's rather suited to you and in which you'll do splendidly. You and your earthlings have been given many opportunities to evolve. You're the ones who have to understand. If you don't, you'll remain what you are now. You will be your own biggest punishment."

I can't see him, but I note the presence of Costantino near me.

"Tainador, how do I close the portal?" I whisper.

"Your Majesty, place both your hands on the mistrofal and recite *mol rim daina mris.*"

"Wait, don't do it!" Anna interjects. "They showed you what they wanted to show you. Those were all illusions. I didn't kill you. I love you and you know I never would."

"Anna, I never said that I saw you kill me. How did you know who my murderer was?"

Anna's eyes fill with tears. She looks down to the ground and falls to her knees on the living room carpet.

Through the portal generated by the mistrofal, my last four words on planet Earth are:

"*Mol rim daina mris.*"

The portal closes.

"Tainador, how do we get out of the Well?" I ask, in the darkness.

"Come along, your Majesty. You have a lot to learn."

Life in Prison

1

I'm innocent. That's what a lot of people will tell you in this god-forsaken place. I, however, truly am innocent. I want to scream it into the void in front of me, but my voice would get lost among thousands of others.

I'm in a cave hollowed out of a rock mass. In front of me, the enormous chasm swallows screams, cries and moans. The prison is in an immense hole that sinks dozens of miles into the ground. The cells are carved into its walls. We're tucked inside of them.

There are hundreds of robots that constantly move about, like bees in a hive. They distribute food in pill-format, take prisoners away, bring in new ones. The unlucky ones are transported on platforms, small flying disks just a few dozen inches in diameter. Keeping your balance and not falling is the first test of survival. When someone gets lost in the void, nobody knows what happens to them.

There are no common areas or outside recreation time. Cells, bars, robots, voices in the shadow, that's it. Well, I also have my cellmate.

His name is Narios. He sleeps and lives in the bunk below mine. Each of us has a little cabinet, a table and a stool. There's a holoprojector in the upper right corner of the room, next to the bars. On the other side there's a single dim light to fight against the darkness of the cell. Beyond a little door there's a sink and a toilet. This is our everyday reality.

2

When I came in on the flying platform, carried by two robots on either side, Narios was sleeping

I had no idea how a prison worked and had never met a prisoner before in my life. The robots left me on the cell floor. I heard the spooky metallic sound of the bars closing behind me. I tried to make out what was in front of me. The beds were on the left wall and the other prisoner slept on one bunk with his head towards the entrance. He snorted and turned over, annoyed by the noise.

My only ideas about this world had come from watching holomovies, when the criminals massacred each other in massive brawls.

He got up and came towards me.

He was bigger, taller and fatter than me, with thinning hair and a week's worth of stubble. He was wearing a frayed, dark blue prison uniform full of patches.

"Hi, I'm Narios."

"Hi, my name is Germil."

"First time here?"

What did that mean? Of course this was my first time here! I had never done anything wrong in my life, I never even stole candy as a kid.

"Yes, of course," I responded.

"So what are you in for?"

I had no idea how to answer. I still hadn't been told why they had brought me here. "I was at home, in the evening. I was putting the kids to bed." I stopped. Thinking about them made me feel a sharp pain in my heart. I went on: "My wife was washing the dishes. I had helped the kids brush their teeth and put their pajamas on and was starting to tell them a story. I heard the doorbell ring and I asked my wife to answer it. I heard her talking to some men, then I heard the footsteps of several people entering my house. I kissed the kids goodnight and went into the living room. I saw two guys sitting and waiting for me, another five standing up. My wife had turned pale and was looking at me, worried. One of the two on the couch showed me a badge from the national security service and told me that I had to follow him, without giving me any other explanations. I reassured my wife, telling her that this must have been some kind of misunderstanding and that I'd come back soon. I had no idea what they wanted from me. They took me to their space shuttle. Once I got in they told me that, for reasons of security, they would have to put me to sleep. When I woke up, they were unloading me on this planet. They told me that due to the crimes committed, I would be kept here while waiting for trial. Then two robots had me get on the platform and brought me here."

My voice was shaking as I finished my story. I still didn't understand what was happening to me.

Narios listened without interrupting. "Were you up to some kind of trick?" he asked in a neutral tone of voice.

What trick? I lived a simple and innocuous life. Every day I went to work in the solar energy plant. When I finished my shift, I went home to my family. I spent my weekends with them on the boat at the lake, watching the birds, swimming and playing on the islands.

"No, I'm an engineer. I don't do anything but work and spend time with my family."

The cell started to spin around me. I had to support myself using one of the bars of the bed.

"Hey, sit down."

Narios brought me one of the two stools. "Maybe you pissed someone off?"

"Well...I don't think I have any enemies. At most there are a few coworkers I don't always get along with, but there have never been any problems."

"I understand. Listen, there are a few things you need to know."

Narios started to explain the simple rules of prison life.

You never get out for any reason, except when you're summoned for trial hearings. You wash yourself with the water in the sink. When they wash your clothes, you wait naked. Food is distributed in pills. Prisoners clean their own cells. You can chat, look at the holobooks, write, do exercises such as push-ups, squats and sit-ups, think and sleep.

If you can't take it any more, it's not too hard to force the cell bars open and take the big jump into the void to end it all down there.

The prison is called Varcoria and is located on Plezis III. It's as simple as it is perfect. Escape is impossible. There's nothing but the cell or death, life or suicide.

3

The days pass, each one the same as the last. I'm caught up in an endless routine: eat, sleep, wash, read, chat.

Narios tells me about his life.

"I got caught with a couple kilos of narcotics. I used and I sold. When I get out of here, I can't wait to go and do some pure plezis." It seems like he really misses the stuff.

"How long have you been here?" I ask him.

"Twenty years."

"What? Are you kidding? How can you spend twenty years in this place? You'd go crazy after just a few days."

"The hardest part," he explains, "is when you finish half of your sentence. I don't know why, but that's when you break down psychologically. Maybe it's because you think of everything that's already happened here and you know there's still more to come.

You live hanging on to every little detail. Your arrival, for example, is an event, you know? Did you notice that, when you got here, everyone in the cells around ours asked if things were alright? I told them yes and for days everyone's been asking about who you are and why you're here. They think back to when they saw you passing by on the platform in front of their cells, how you looked, the expression on your face. It seems like something insignificant, but here it's what life is made of."

I listen to his words, incredulously. Narios is like an animal in a cage. He moves with a self-assurance and naturalness that makes me uncomfortable. He seems to belong here, like he's at home. I'm frightened to see him so adjusted to this reality. I realize that after twenty years, there's really no other way.

"Once in a while one of us goes nuts," he tells me, "and we try to help him. Generally, cellmates try to do everything they can to keep morale high. Neighbors will give advice. But sometimes you close in on yourself and don't come out again. Everything loses its meaning. You can't see the point anymore and jumping into the void seems like a liberation. When one of us goes, we don't talk about anything else for weeks."

Talking is the only thing these people have. The voices from one cell to the other create an incessant buzz.

There's a holoprojector in the cell that transmits tens of thousands of channels. I'd like to catch a movie or the news every once in a while but, whenever we start watching something, Narios always wants to talk. He doesn't seem able to focus on anything for very long. Maybe he's just excited by the novelty of my company.

"Is this what you thought prison life would be like?" he asks me one day.

"Well, I only knew what I saw in the holomovies – lots of scenes of violence and oppression and dramatic prison breaks."

"Every once in a while a few cellmates go at it, but for the most part people here try to stay positive. As for prison breaks, it's impossible to climb over the walls. There are hundreds of robots rolling up and down all the time. If someone is crazy enough to try, they'll only get a few yards up before they're caught."

I tell him about my life and my work. I try not to say too much or give precise information on where I live or which solar plant I work in. From the holomovies, I learned that you never give very detailed information about yourself when you're in prison.

"You're not a criminal. I know people like me. Everyone here says they're more or less innocent, but we know who really is. You're not like us. You don't belong here. You'll see, they'll make you suffer while waiting for the trial, but then, when you go to the hearing, you'll explain who you are and, after a few days, they'll let you out.

Sometimes they just want to be sure that, if you know something, you won't waste their time and when they ask you'll spill the beans immediately. If they take someone like you and shut him up in here, I'm sure that after a few days of hell, you'd be ready to blurt it all out."

He speaks confidently. After twenty years of this life he seems to understand how the legal system works. I hope he's right.

I try not to think about my family. When they're on my mind, my heart feels like it's going to explode. It's probably even more difficult for them than it is for me. At least I know that I'm alive, that I'm okay and that I can hang in there. I wonder what Sofia, my wife, knows and how she's holding up. What did she tell our children? She probably said that I was on a business trip. Sometimes the company organizes training courses in other places. Those are the only times I'm ever away from them.

I'm dying to hug them again!

I think constantly about what I'll say during the hearing. I want to explain my job at the plant precisely, trying to be as clear and as exhaustive as possible with every detail. The judge should understand that I've never done anything bad.

I tell Narios about it, and he reassures me. "I believe you. Whenever something happens, they lock up a ton of people. When they find out who it was, they let the others out." He pauses. "There's no way in hell you belong in prison. When they figure it all out, they'll let you out of here."

It seems like a perverse mechanism, but now I'm ready to accept any condition just to go home. However, a thousand doubts come over me: what if the reason why I'm here has to do with something that happened at the plant? And what if someone had unjustly accused me to cover up what they did themselves? And what if, without even knowing it, I had really done something wrong?

If you throw an innocent man in prison, he'll start to doubt that he's indeed innocent.

I remember when I was in elementary school, a classmate drew all over the walls with crayons. When the teacher grilled him, he accused me of doing it. The teacher punished me before I knew what I was being accused of. And after a while I even started to wonder if I was really guilty.

After a few days, a robot comes to the cell and calls for me. I get up and go to the bars, my heart racing. I'm terrorized by the idea of getting bad news.

"Your hearing before Judge Artis Majioris will take place in two days, on October twenty-seventh two thousand one hundred twenty-seven," the robot tells me in a neutral tone of voice.

For hours, all I can do is think about the drudge's twenty words.

4

I repeat over and over what I want to say at the hearing.

The day finally comes. I carefully groom myself in the bathroom. There's a small, slightly cracked mirror. I rinse the standard issue comb under the water in the sink and adjust my blond hair until my hairdo is perfect. I shave. My blue eyes examine my sharp jawline: a perfect shave, too bad the judge isn't a lady. Under normal circumstances, you could call me somewhat charming.

Sitting on a stool, I wait for the robot to arrive. To distract me, Narios tells me about his job, his official job. He was a cook – a really good cook, according to him. I can't concentrate much on his words, but I like the feeling of having him at my side.

Two robots, carrying an empty platform between them, fly up and stop in front of the cell bars, which open automatically. I get up and walk towards them. I feel their hands latch on to my arms, to keep me from falling. Silently, we begin to rise.

I look at the faces of the prisoners whose voices I've been listening to for days. Their eyes are all glued on me. They know that my life will be decided in the next few hours.

The other robots continue moving in front of the cells. They carry along little boxes that contain food and medicine. A few accompany other prisoners whose eyes have the same incredulous and frightened gaze that I imagine I have, too. The sequence of cells goes on infinitely, both upwards and downwards.

After a few minutes, a perfectly smooth frame about 150 yards long per side appears on the wall. There's an opening in the middle of it, a short corridor and a metallic door. We're heading there. Once we go through the door, we walk down a long corridor with metal walls, floor and ceiling. We walk in through a second door and enter a circular room about twenty yards in diameter. The walls, ceiling and floor are white. There's a chair in the middle.

"Have a seat. The hearing will begin within three minutes," one of the two robots informs me. They leave me alone. *The artificial intelligence programmers working on these androids certainly gave them the gift of brevity*, I think with a bitter smile.

I walk to the middle of the room. I sit down and wait.

The walls and floor disappear. I'm in the middle of a courtroom. I know this technology: it's a type of virtual reality where the scene is a projection and the objects are holograms. It's indistinguishable from a real place, as long as you don't try to touch the objects.

The room is empty. The judge enters after a few moments. He's young, with short, dark hair parted on the right. He looks at a holobook. "Good morning," he tells me, without lifting his eyes. In his courtroom, I think, I must appear as a hologram.

"I'm Artemio Geracis. I'm here to record your deposition. Ready to proceed?" *Artemio Geracis? Who is he? Where's Judge Artis Majioris?* I study the individual in front of me, he looks like a paper-pusher.

I make an effort. "Good morning, your Honor. I was informed that the hearing would be held in the presence of Judge Artis Majioris."

Error! I'm sure I annoyed him with my statement. And he makes me understand that. He lifts his eyes up. "The Judge can't be present at this hearing because of other commitments. Your deposition will be sent to him telematically. Please proceed."

"Pardon me, during my detention I was not informed of the reason why I was detained. Would it be possible to have more information on the reasons why I was incarcerated?" Now I seem to have a formal and proper attitude. My request is more than obvious. In theory there's no reason why he'd be irritated.

"Listen, it's not my job to provide you with any information. I'm here to take your deposition. If you don't want to proceed, I'll report that you preferred to abstain."

I'm terrified. The situation has become even more absurd and surreal. Is this a dream or a joke? Meanwhile the paper-pusher has raised his head and is staring at me, impatient.

"Judge, can I appoint an attorney to assist me?"

"Your legal assistance will be provided by a staff attorney, and your family will be notified of the appointment. In any case, you are not allowed to communicate with your legal counsel for reasons of security."

Security? What kind of mess did I get mixed up in? I don't know what I've been accused of, or who my attorney is, and I have to make a deposition on I don't know what.

I feel like I'm losing but I make an effort to describe who I am and what I do, what my tasks are at work, who I hang out with. I show that there are no grey areas in my life. I try to give a complete

85

picture. I try to understand from his expression if I'm convincing.

"Are you through?" he asks me, without showing any emotion.

"Yes," I nod.

The courtroom disappears. The circular room is once again white. The door behind me opens. I turn my head. The silent robots appear beside me. Thinking about the cell I'm probably returning to makes me want to vomit.

5

"Everything okay, bro?"

Narios' eyes are sweet and paternal. He started calling me 'bro', who knows why. I want to say yes. I tell him what happened. I'm a little down.

"Come on, don't worry," he says to cheer me up. I can't be consoled.

"Hey, Germil, what's with the sad face? You said everything you had to say. You explained who you are and what you know. As soon as the Judge hears your deposition, he'll realize there's been a mistake and you'll get out of here. So you'll find out whose ass you need to kick for getting you caught up in this mess for two weeks."

Narios is kind. I hug him.

The days pass and every time a robot comes near our cell, a wave of terror washes over me. Why am I so convinced that bad news is on its way?

I hear from the legal system a few days later.

The robot stops in front of the bars. My heart leaps out of my chest. Narios puts a hand on my shoulder, shakes my hand and smiles.

"Hey, bro, it's over."

"Thanks, Narios, whatever happens, I'm really grateful for everything you've done."

"Germil Isiek, you've been sentenced to seven earth years and two earth months to be served in the Varcoria prison on Plezis III. Do you wish to appeal? Any legal expenses will be paid by your family, subject to their approval."

The smile on Narios' face disappears.

"Yes, yes," I babble. "I want to appeal."

The robot silently moves away from the cell.

I stretch out on the cot. I thought I'd feel bad, but I actually don't feel anything.

Narios leaves me alone.

I'm calm. I'm not overcome by sorrow. *Seven years and two months.* I don't feel rage or discomfort. Now I know what I'm in for. I feel like a soldier who, when wounded in battle, doesn't feel real pain until he's sure that he's safe in the trench.

I lie on the cot for hours. Irrelevant, tiny, scattered thoughts cross my mind. I force myself to not think about my family.

6

New day, same routine. I thought that I would be overcome by pain, but still nothing. It's as if I was anesthetized. Actually I don't know what I feel.

Two robots stop in front of the bars. I go out as I am. This time, unshaven and with messy hair. *What do they want from me?*

We fly up and pass the opening that leads to the hearing room. We go up further. *How high is this place?* The walls are now smooth, we've left the lower cells. There are fewer robots up here. I see above me the large cupola that separates the chasm of the prison from the planet's toxic atmosphere. Just twenty yards below the top, we go through an opening, similar to the first one. Even the corridor we walk down is identical to the one that led to the courtroom. The robots stop in front of a door. I understand that I need to go forward and enter a rectangular space, with metallic walls and white furniture, ceiling and floor. The design is sparse and minimalistic.

On the left, two armchairs and a little sofa form a sitting room. At the back of the room there's a desk with a pair of two office chairs in front of it. I see a woman with long, smooth, dark hair down to her shoulders absorbed in reading. She's dressed in a slightly dated grey, simple suit with a white shirt and black low-heeled shoes. Her face is slightly rotund, and she's not wearing much makeup, if any at all. She's pretty.

"Germil Isiek, I presume."

I observe her silently.

"Please, have a seat."

I sit down.

"Among thousands of prisoners, we don't have many engineers at your level. As a matter of fact, I think you're the only one." A smile slips across her face.

Who is this woman? And why is she smiling at me like that? She seems like the kind of woman who has a lot to hide.

"You're in luck," I respond. "Now if you have a problem with your solar panels, there's someone here who can take a look at it."

I don't laugh at my joke, because it wasn't funny. She, however, lets out a shrill peal.

"I think the robots take care of the maintenance around here, actually, I've never worried about it."

I start to really feel irritated and fear that my eyes betray my disgust.

"I'm the Director of Varcoria, Ally Bristis," she says. She noticed my glaring expression and wants to make our respective positions clear, but immediately resumes her little smile.

In return, I pretend that this is a normal conversation.

"It's a pleasure to meet you, Ms. Bristis." I respond, in a formal tone of voice.

"Six years and two months," she says, thoughtfully. "Your appeal should come through in eight weeks."

"Well, in the end, it's not too bad around here," I say, ironically.

Is she really a fool or is she only pretending to be one? Maybe it's just prison policy to torture each detainee with her stupidity.

"Alright, we'll have an opportunity to talk more later, but now I have a few things to take care of. Have a nice day."

Now she's really being a jerk. Does she realize that I have to go back to a cell?

As we go back down, I wonder if it's worse to spend part of my life in a cell, or an entire life as stupid as Ally Bristis. After all, one day I'll get out of here. She'll probably work in this prison all her life.

7

I tell Narios about the surreal encounter. He remains silent, like he does every time he can't figure something out. From his expression, I understand that meeting with the Director is a rather unusual thing for a detainee to do.

"Well, maybe it's a good sign, bro."

He always tries to emphasize the positive aspect of every situation. I feel very selfish: even if he constantly strives to make me feel better, I really don't think much of him. But I'm beginning to like him a little.

A deadly boredom assails me. The routine completely floors me. Narios tries to keep my morale up any way he can. All I want to do is read. The holobooks are the only thing that capture my interest and help me escape from all of this. Narios, however, interrupts me constantly. I almost feel guilty for how irritable I am with him. I know that he does it because he wants to be close to me, but I really need to throw myself into reading in order to forget about everything.

I hear the bars open, I turn around and see two robots, immobile. Trying to contain the feeling that some bad news is on its way, I go towards them and step out onto the platform. We start rising upwards. *Let's hope I don't come back from this!*

Instead, they take me right to the Director.

She's busy doing something at the desk. Then she looks at me and, with her big fake smile, encourages me to loathe her even more.

"Hi, Germil. Please, have a seat on the couch. I can call you Germil, right?"

No, actually! I think. We're not friends and I doubt we ever will be, but for now I abstain from telling her so.

"Hi, Ally."

"Can I offer you something to drink? Actually we don't have a whole lot here. Wait, I'll order something."

She comes and sits down on the sofa, next to me. Her steps are calm but a little too controlled.

"I saw the deposition you made at the hearing. You don't know how sorry I am that you ended up here."

I don't comment. I think my silence is starting to embarrass her.

A robot brings us two tall, narrow glasses. Her glass is full of a shiny green drink, and mine is a bright blue. I've never seen any beverages like these before.

"I imagine this would be a pleasant change of pace compared to the food pills and water from the sink."

Well, you're the Director, if you want to serve me a nice plate of pasta with a good bottle of wine, go right ahead.

She lifts her glass towards me. "Cheers!" She gives me a foolish smile.

"Cheers," I respond.

I take a sip and immediately feel looser, at peace, calm, a pleasant sensation. The room is warm and welcoming. I wonder if the beverage is some kind of drug, but I've never tried any and wouldn't know how to guess. I feel really good.

"That's just what you needed, right?" she asks me.

"Not bad, Ally. Not bad at all."

She smiles. *What the hell am I doing?* asks a little voice from somewhere inside of me.

"Let's talk a little bit about you," she says.

The voice inside of me doesn't want to say anything, but I reel on for several minutes about everything that comes to mind about my life. The words seem to come out on their own. She wants to know about my wife Sofia, and I tell her how we met, the engagement, our marriage, the kids. Ally looks at me, interested. Talking about my family now isn't painful. I feel like I'm at dinner with friends.

Ally's legs are crossed. Her foot bounces up and down. *Are those the same black shoes she wore the last time?* I wonder. When I lift my eyes again, I realize she noticed what I was gazing at.

"Have a seat on the floor, you'll be more comfortable." She smiles.

On the floor? I don't usually sit on the ground.

I get up from the sofa and start to bend my legs. *I don't want to do this, why am I doing this?* I think as I get down on the ground, my head near her shoe.

I look around, searching for something to help me understand. *The drink!* I look at the glass that contained the blue beverage. Then I turn towards the Director. She says: "Nothing wrong with a little fun, right?"

I'm not having fun, but the sensations in my body are pleasant.

"If you like my shoe, do whatever you want with it."

I don't want to do anything with it. The tip of her shoe comes towards my lips.

"You want to kiss it, don't you?"

Yes, I mean, no! I have no idea what I want to do.

The effects of the drink seem to intensify in my body. I put my lips on her shoe. I kiss it in several places. I rise towards her calf. I stop. *Maybe I should lick it?* I stick out my tongue and start to run it down the leather of her shoe. I look up at her, she's nodding. I set myself to the task at hand. She points her toe upwards. I look at her, surprised. She nods, indicating I should go on. Her approval makes me more enthusiastic. I pass my tongue vigorously along the sole of her shoe. It's like I'm trying to clean it. "Take it off..."

Her bare foot seems like a conquest to me. There are no more contradictory little voices inside of me. With my lips and tongue, I go up her calf, reach her knee and linger along the inside of her thighs. I don't dare go further. She raises her skirt a little with her hands and then places a palm on my head. I let her push me. With her other hand, she pulls her panties aside a little. I start to really get into it. She lets out soft, throaty cries. Then she places a foot on my forehead and pushes me away. With one finger, she opens the buttons of my uniform, from the neck down to the waist. I don't understand. I go back to my first position. She puts her right foot behind my neck and again pulls me between her thighs. I see her place one hand behind the arm of the sofa. I realize that she's holding a whip in her hand.

My tongue and my lips go back to pleasuring her.

The first lash arrives unexpectedly, strong and extremely painful. She screams, apparently out of her mind with pleasure. I stop because of the pain.

"Don't you dare stop. Continue!"

Her imperious tone forces me back to work without a second thought.

The other lashes arrive in a violent, steadily increasing rhythm. The pain almost makes me faint. My back seems to collapse. I feel the blood trickle down my skin. But I don't stop doing what I'm doing and she, with every lash, seems full of a savage joy. The rhythm of her hand increasingly intensifies, just like her pleasure. She explodes in an intense orgasm and shakes with violent tremors.

I stop. Her screams of pleasure seem further and further away.

The image of her skin covered with pleasure and sweat starts to grow fuzzy. The pain in my back disappears. I feel my forehead hit the floor when my body collapses, senseless.

8

I feel the shape of a pillow under my right cheek. The pain is atrocious in my back, it seems like I'm in a haze. I try to figure out where I am. I open my eyes: I see the cot and part of the greyish, dirty wall. *I'm still in this filthy cell.* I turn my face. The movement stimulates the muscles of my back, which scream out in pain. Narios notices this. He turns and smiles at me. He grabs the stool and sits down next to me.

"Hey, bro, what did they do to you? Two robots carried you into the cell, you were unconscious and stayed that way for two days. The wounds are a little better now. I tried to do what I could, but we only have rags and water here."

"Narios..."

It hurts even to speak.

"That bitch."

My voice is barely above a whisper.

"The Director? Her again? What happened?"

"She made me drink something blue...I don't know what it was...but afterwards it felt like I was...a robot...under her command."

He looks at me, perplexed. I tell him what happened. He listens without interrupting, his face darkens.

"No, bro, shit, I'm sorry! I'm really sorry! Why did she pick you? We're all monsters here, human wrecks, criminals, racketeers, dealers, murderers, junkies, thieves! Why you? I don't know what to say, bro. Come here!"

I look at him, terrorized. He understands that maybe this isn't the time for a fraternal hug.

Over the next few days, Narios tends to my wounds, soothes them and keeps them clean, helps me with everything. I stay lying down, but every once in a while I pull myself up to a sitting position.

After two more weeks I feel like I'm almost normal. I start to do push-ups, sit-ups and other exercises to stay in shape. In the mirror, I can see there are still a few scars. *If I could only get my hands on that subspecies of a bitch!*

Two silent robots stop in front of the bars of my cell. *Her again, I know it is!*

She waits for me, standing a few feet away from the door, with an apprehensive look on her face.

"How are you?" she asks, in no uncertain terms.

"Well..."

"I monitored how you were doing from the video surveillance of your cell. I'm *so* sorry about your wounds. Good thing Narios was there to take care of you. He didn't take his eyes off of you from the moment they brought you back to the cell!"

"I don't think he had anything else to do."

"Come on, you understand what I mean!" she says in a friendly tone, patting my arm.

Is she insane? Isn't she the one who whipped me until I almost dropped dead?

"Maybe it was worth it, though, right?" she asks me, tenderly taking my hand and bringing me to the sofa.

"For what?"

She acts embarrassed. "You were good, really good. And your Director really likes you. So we had to wait a little longer so you could get better." The seductive tone again.

I don't understand if I'm dealing with some sort of evil genius, a schizophrenic criminal or a complete imbecile.

"And," she continues, "I think that you really liked it too, right, Germil?"

"We need to get things straight, dear Ally." I emphasize her name. "I have a wife, two children and a nice life. All of a sudden you locked me up in this hell as punishment for I have no idea what. One fine day the director, *you,* decided to whip me unconscious, leaving me incapable of movement for days with a back that looks like a battlefield. What part of this do you think I find pleasant?"

She's offended, and starts to pout. What the hell do I care if she's pouting? Why doesn't she kill herself and leave me alone?

"Okay, maybe Ally exaggerated a little, but I'm not that experienced. I mean, I'm a beginner. I don't like having to wait all this time between meetings either. Can we call a truce?" Her tone and words are a mixture between a toddler and a crazy friend. Her words *between meetings* set off an alarm inside of me.

"Do you want another drink?" she asks me.

"Ally, please, leave me alone. I have to spend six years in this place and I'm counting the days that separate me from the end of this punishment, since the appeal isn't looking good. Please let me go on with my miserable existence. I won't give you any problems, I'll be a model prisoner. I won't tell anyone about what happened. Please, I have a family, children..."

My words make her think. Maybe something inside of her is moving.

"Germil, listen, that beverage isn't an offer. *Do you want* to drink something?" She has the sympathetic tone of someone who's doing you a big favor.

The robot brings our glasses to the coffee table in front of the sofa and stops a few feet away from us.

"Go ahead. I'm sure we won't have problems with Germil." She lifts her glass. "Cheers, dear."

I drink.

I suddenly feel comfortable with Ally. Now the room, furniture and decoration seem pleasant and welcoming.

Something tells me this is all an illusion, but I don't pay attention to it. If it is, it's incredibly nice. I forgot about the cell and my other life. I feel good, relaxed.

Ally goes to her desk and comes back with a pack of cigarettes. She lights one. *Wow! I want to smoke one too!* I observe her lips, closed around the filter. She breathes in deeply. She holds the smoke inside. She exhales. I don't know how to resist the temptation.

She knows I'm looking at her. "Do you smoke? Do you want one?"

Do I smoke? I don't remember ever doing it.

I look at her, a little surprised. She smiles, satisfied. "You don't remember if you smoke?"

"I don't know."

"Don't worry, Germil. These drinks not only make you a tiny bit more inclined to accept my requests, but they also blur your past a bit. This way you feel better, right?"

Oh yes, that's true. I feel really good.

"Listen," she continues. "You need to earn the cigarette, okay?"

Sure, no problem!

"So now I'd like to have you lie down right here, in front of me."

I lie down in front of her, my face under her shoes, which are bright blue with stiletto heels. I remember her shoes were black last time. She brings the tip of one heel down into my mouth. I start to lick it, avidly. She's obviously pleased. She puts the heel between my lips and I let it go far down into my mouth. Then she gets up, takes a step towards the table, puts out her cigarette, turns around and puts the heel again between my lips, balancing on her other leg. She starts to push it down harder, towards my throat. It hurts. I want to vomit, and I can't breathe. I give her a begging look, hoping she'll help me. She stares at me and pushes down harder. I feel that I can't hold on any longer. Finally she takes her foot off of my throat.

"You're so handsome when you suffer for me."

She kneels down next to me. I feel her hands in my hair.

"This is what you want, right?"

I think so, but I'm not sure.

"Yes, Ally."

"I want to hear you say it to me."

I don't know what exactly to tell her.

"Tell me!" she repeats, insistently.

I have to respond.

"I want to serve you. I want to be under you. I want to learn how to fulfill your desires. I want to be whipped and stepped on and beaten up. I want to be an object in your hands. I want to feel you pour out all of your violence over me. I want to hit the limits of everything I can bear and go beyond them."

I can't control the words that are streaming out of my mouth. Ally is in ecstasy. "Good, Germil, you'll be mine. You'll be my little toy, forever."

She kisses me, biting my lips. I taste blood mixed with saliva. She unbuttons my uniform. Her nails dig into the skin of my back. She continues kissing me, biting me, scratching me.

"Take it all off!"

As I take off the uniform, she gets out of her business suit. She lies on the floor, on her back. She invites me to get on top of her. When I penetrate her, I close my eyes and moan with pleasure. We start to make love passionately. Her hands are still on my back. She can't hold back any longer and scratches me manically.

"Lift up your head. Keep it up."

She screams with joy with the first slap. She seems full of an ecstatic pleasure and continues slapping me, harder and harder. Her rhythm is frenetic. She's going out of her mind with pleasure. Her forehead is beaded with sweat from the effort. My blood starts to drip onto her neck and face. She brings her other hand up to her lips.

The rhythm of the slaps becomes frenetic. She reaches orgasm, screaming savagely. I come with her.

She gently pushes me off of her body. She nods towards the little table. She picks up her cigarettes and lights one, still relaxed. I'm sitting, my back hurts and so does my face. "You deserved it." She offers me a cigarette, which I light. I like smoking. It's a strange feeling, it's relaxing.

I feel like something is wrong.

9

"Bro, what's the name of the plant where you used to work?"

"I don't know, Narios, I don't remember."

"How could you not remember?! You worked there your whole life!"

I don't even remember the name of my daughter's school, or most of my coworkers. I have a vague idea of where I used to take the family to eat every Saturday evening. The memories are blurred, far away, vague.

"Narios, I don't know what to do."

"Germil, you need to stop drinking that stuff."

The Director usually calls for me every three or four days.

"I can't! Once I refused and she made the robots force it down my throat."

"That whore doesn't even have a heart! Try talking to her again. You said that she likes you, in a way."

"No, I said that she said she adored her toy and can't live without it. She doesn't give a damn about me. She wants her sex slave, her horse to ride, the one that brings her pleasure."

"Germil, you need to be careful. If you lose your memory, you lose everything."

As we speak, the robots come towards the bars to get me and take me to her. When I return, Narios is pale.

"Germil, the hearing..."

"What?" What is he talking about?

"The robots came by to take you to the hearing for your appeal!"

No, it can't be! I'm still under the aftereffects of the blue drink, but I feel the cell floor collapse.

There's no way the Director didn't know about the hearing. Did she call for me on purpose? I can see the fake, incredulous look she'll give me when I ask her.

My cellmate and I remain silent.

"The attorney was there!" Narios exclaims, triumphant. "Your family must have agreed to pay for your legal assistance. They must have taken care of everything. Even if you weren't present, I'm sure it went well."

I lower my eyes. I feel lost.

"Germil, don't give up now. It'll be over soon, I can feel it. I know it will. Just have faith, a few more days and this time it'll be over for good."

I don't know what I'd do without him.

However, as I suspected, Narios wasn't quite right. In fact, a few days later the robot announces:

"Germil Isiek, you've been sentenced to eighteen earth years and six earth months to be served in the Varcoria prison on Plezis III. Do you wish to make an appeal in the Court of Cassation? Any legal expenses will be paid by your family, subject to their approval."

The same words as last time, but my mind can't process the number of years of the sentence.

"How many years?" I ask the robot.

"Eighteen earth years and six earth months. Would you like to hear the number in days, hours, minutes or the conversion into years of another planet?"

"No, no, thanks. I think I understood. Yes, I want to appeal."

I turn towards Narios. He's sitting on the stool, with his head in his hands, crying.

I get up and hug him. I want to reassure him: "Come on, we'll find a solution."

"No, there is no solution. Sorry, Germil. You just got the worst news of your life and you shouldn't be over here trying to console me." He's crying desperately. "This is impossible! What the hell kind of system is this? They're murdering you!"

"Narios, I'm alive. There are other options. The Court of Cassation is another kind of court, with other judges. I'm sure my wife will do everything she can to get me out of here."

"Sorry, Germil. I'm by your side, I have been since the beginning. Forgive me, you shouldn't have to deal with my whimpering."

"Narios, you've been here for twenty years and you're a really good person. If I learn how to be as great a person as you've become in eighteen years, then these won't be years spent in vain."

Nobody has ever bothered to try and erase Narios' memory.

10

"No, it's okay, I don't need any drinks, I'm here to do what you want and I always will."

Ally looks at me, proud.

"Germil, do you really mean it?"

"Ally, my place is at your side, under your feet, under your whip, between your thighs. My only desire is to not have any other desires aside from yours. When I'm in my cell, I only think of when I'll be with you again. I want to be an object in your hands. You can use me and throw me away as you please. I want to feel your will replace my own. I'm yours. I belong to you."

"Germil, I adore you. Do you know how happy you made me today? Good, I'm glad that you don't want to drink that stuff any more. It does strange things to your long-term memory. It's better this way."

Her black knee-high boots look great. She's a beautiful woman.

This time we only fuck, without any torture. She lies down on the little table. Her head and hair hang over the edge. I take her vigorously. The heels of her boots push into my thighs. Afterwards, we smoke together.

"I don't know what I'd do without you, Germil. Nobody has ever made me feel so much pleasure."

I'm curious to know if she used to fuck other prisoners before me, but I'd rather not ask.

"And I'm very happy to hear your decision. You know, you'd never have gotten out of here anyway. At least now I know that you're staying here out of your own free will."

I kiss her, passionately. *What the fuck are you saying, you ugly bitch?* What does that mean, that I'd never have gotten out of here anyway?

I smile at her, as if I'm in love. "Being with you is the best thing that ever happened to me and I can't imagine life any other way."

"I did help move things along a little..." She smiles, like a bratty little kid. "Well, unfortunately, considering the serious errors you made and your terrible behavior in prison, the second-level Judge decided to triple your sentence. And it seems to me that, after looking at what you've been up to lately, the Court of Cassation will give you a life sentence."

I open my eyes wide and give her a passionate kiss. "You're diabolical!" I whisper.

"It's getting late. I think you need to go back to your cell. Um...you're doing just a little too *well* today. Tomorrow I'll have you picked up a little earlier so I can have more time to take care of you."

"Did you get the anal dilator you ordered?" I ask her. "I can't wait!"

"You little pig, I told you you'll have to wait until next week. You can't find these things everywhere. And there are always other methods, as you know full well!"

She kisses me tenderly and the two robots materialize to take me outside.

I'll never get out of here! I'm in the hands of an insane person and a legal system created and run by her peers.

I had a wife – this I remember – and two beautiful children who I loved to death. She was named Sofia, I think. I can't remember their names, exactly. I think I was an engineer. I worked somewhere that had something to do with energy. I had good friends, but I don't remember any of them now. Narios and I are really close. He's the closest human being to me and I love him like a brother. Maybe if he doesn't see me come back, he'll think I was released. Nobody knows what's going on down in the chasm. He'll always wonder if I'm happy, at home with my family, celebrating a promotion or my kids' good grades from school.

This is what I think about as I cross the short corridor that leads to the platform. I jump up and feel the hands of the robots grab my arms. We fly down. When it seems like we're more or less in the middle of the giant hole, I rip their arms off of me and let myself fall into the void. *I'll never see my family again, I'll never get my life back. But now at least that shitty psychopath won't have me either.*

As I fall into the void, everything seems to slow down. I see the cells, thousands of cells carved into the rock. I can still make out, in the shadows, the outlines of the faces of prisoners, zoo animals that pace back and forth in an existence that's no longer worth anything. Most of them will never get out of here and those that do leave will always have this place in their hearts. It's life in prison for everyone. The human soul is destroyed here. All that's left is a black hole in your mind that will suck away your energy for the rest of your existence.

I feel that, just a few hundred feet below, the walls will end, and so will my life.

Suddenly I feel the will to live. I don't care how or where. I just want to live. The thoughts vanish. Everything accelerates. My heart races and seems to jump out of my chest. I see, out of the corner of my eye, two robots flying towards me. *Do they want to save me?*

Then everything goes dark. I'm dead.

11

"Germil, darling. Germil... Gegi, are you awake?"

Gegi? Only she calls me that. *Yes, I'm awake, but how can I tell her?* Everything is dark. I try to open my eyes. Do I still have eyes? Yes, I do.

The face of my wife Sofia seems to light up the room. I turn towards her hand, which caresses my cheek. The scent of flowers from our garden and soap. I look at her. She's more beautiful than ever: blonde, shiny short hair. She's wearing the pearl necklace I gave her. It was for...I don't remember.

But Sofia, yes, I could never forget her. She's the woman who gave birth to our children, the woman I promised my life to.

"My darling," I tell her, my eyes full of tears. "I thought I'd never see you again. I love you."

She kisses me passionately, then looks around her, worried. "But you need to hurry now. You need to go to them. They said they can't wait and that I'd have to wake you up." Them?

"Who are they? What do they want?"

I sit up on the bed. She hands me a pair of jeans and a t-shirt. *Are these my clothes?* Yes, they are. Sofia bought me the jeans and I got the t-shirt from a market near the lake. *The lake?* The one where the whole family would go on days when it was gorgeous outside.

"Kids!" Her voice sounds like music to my ears.

They run into the room like two furies.

"Daddy, daddy, you came back!" the older one says, jumping on me with a momentum that makes me fall back onto the bed. The little one hugs my thigh, full of emotion.

"Daddy, you're finished with work, right? You're not leaving again, right?"

"Children," Sofia interrupts, "your father needs to go see his friends and then he'll be with you as long as you want."

They hand me the t-shirt that fell on the floor and a pair of socks. They bring me shoes and a belt, carefully chosen by the older of the two.

"Alright, now let him be, go play. Daddy will be there soon." They're not too convinced but they follow their mom's instructions. I don't remember them being so obedient.

When I walk into the living room, a man and a woman stand up and hold out their hands. He's wearing a grey suit. His face is square, he's balding, short and a little overweight. She's wearing a blouse and a blue skirt down to the middle of her calves and is holding a holobook. Her chin is small, her cheeks sunken and her nose long. Her skin is opaque and her hair tinged with grey.

I shake the woman's hand first, then the man's, and invite them to sit down.

"Mr. Isiek, we have a lot of information to give you and not a lot of time. Please listen carefully and stop us anytime something isn't sufficiently clear. If you don't follow these rules, it could cost you dearly."

His face shows no emotion as he speaks. I feel like there's a prison robot in front of me.

"We were appointed by Judge Majistis to give you the instructions you'll need to follow for the rest of your life. You were declared mentally ill after your suicide attempt. The prison guards came to your aid before you hit the ground and brought you to the hospital where, upon the judge's orders, a few devices were implanted in you to prevent such a situation from happening again.

You are under orders to resume your position in society. Your new status requires a few small limitations to your freedom. The new contraptions in your body will help protect your safety. The first is connected to the optic nerve. It records everything your eyes see and sends it to the server. Automatic processing of this data will allow us to know what you're doing and be sure that you won't try to commit suicide again, or other crimes for that matter."

Incredulous, I try to say something. The pudgy guy raises his hand. *But shouldn't I stop them if I have any questions?*

"Questions at the end, please. In the past, there have been a few cases of mentally ill people who, preferring to do without this type of control, spent several months blind. If you, while awake, spend too much time with your eyes closed, a team will be sent to check on you and take any measures necessary.

Secondly, you are expressly forbidden from contacting anyone you know from prison or your legal problems.

The second device was implanted in your throat to record every word. The processor will automatically monitor this data to make sure you're not violating this regulation.

The third device is in your heart. If it detects a danger you're creating for yourself or others, it will trigger a drastic and urgent intervention. The device will block your heartbeat without further warning.

Naturally, these three devices will continuously communicate your exact position. That's it. We have a few minutes for questions."

"You're telling me that, after I tried to kill myself, I was set free despite being sentenced to eighteen years in prison?" I try to adjust to his lack of expression.

"You're not free. You're on probation."

"So everyone who attempts suicide in prison gets the same treatment?"

"I'm not authorized to provide that sort of information."

"Okay, let's talk about the devices. Are you sure that the data sent from my body will be processed correctly and won't make me die from a heart attack while I'm fishing at the lake?"

"Mr. Isiek, these systems were developed by the most respected legal experts. There is no doubt that they will function properly and there has never been a case of error."

"And how would you verify a case of error?"

"We are not authorized to provide that sort of information."

The woman still hasn't opened her mouth. She listens, impassible.

"One last thing. Can you tell me why I was imprisoned in the first place?"

"The appropriate clarifications were surely provided in Varcoria, on Plezis III. It's not our job to get into that subject."

"I assure you that I received absolutely no information on the subject. I must insist that you answer my question," I answer.

"In this case I suggest that you contact the office of Judge Majioris. Remember, however, that your status prevents you from discussing the matter with others, including your wife, children and attorney. Is that all?"

Yes, that's all. Not even a telepath could get anything out of these two bureaucrats.

"Thank you very much. Goodbye."

"Goodbye," they both respond. Now I know the woman has a voice, too.

As soon as our *guests* leave, I head straight towards the kids' bedroom.

"Where are my little kittens?" I get down on my hands and knees to catch them in a big bear hug. They raise their heads from their game, spread out all over the floor.

"Daddy!"

Forms of Love

1

I've chased her halfway around the galaxy, but I can't do it anymore. I'm tired, in pain, worn out. It was all in vain. I feel like I just wasted the last few years of my life, the ones I've spent doing nothing but running after her.

I'm a police officer. My successful career has made me famous.

I've appeared in the news on civilized planets throughout the galaxy so many times I've lost count. They gave me the toughest cases and put me in charge of catching the worst criminals. Then they asked me to nab her.

For me, it was a job just like any other: bring one insipid mutant female to the maximum security prison.

After routing out bands of criminals who leeched off the inhabitants of their native planets, I thought it would be the easiest job imaginable. I figured I'd be in the news again, her in handcuffs, me smiling.

Now I'm still in this mess, on a spaceship that's badly in need of maintenance, ready to eject me in a rescue module once it finally falls apart.

And once again, she's ahead of me. It's almost as if she can anticipate my every move. I think she's toying with me.

It's all a game: she lets me get one step away from her and, just when I'm sure I've got her, she loves to flee from me.

It's like she enjoys feeling my breath on her neck.

She's a mutant, she can take on any form at any moment.

In theory, this shouldn't help her all that much: we police officers are equipped with biometric scanners and wide-range DNA detectors. No matter where she goes, her genes can be picked up by local readers. I know when she touches down on a planet.

"Captain, look!"

Eianus is talking. He's a young police officer they recently paired me up with. The FoW, or Federation of Worlds, is so exasperated with my failure that it decided to send me this kid. Tall, blonde, blue eyes, a perfect university record, first in every advanced class of the police training course, he's got a thorough knowledge of the most modern technologies.

"It looks like Ipsia suddenly changed course," Eianus says.

We're hot on her heels, if you could say that about pursuing someone who's still a few light years away.

In the middle of the room, between Eianus and I, there's a hologram we can use to trace the position of Ipsia's spaceship as well as many other objects moving through space.

"It went into the Mx-311 solar system. From what I see, the only planet she could land on is Mx-311-d," Einaus adds.

"What kind of planet is that?" I ask.

"It's a quarter sea and three quarters emerged land, covered with thick vegetation. Life is still in a primitive and wild stage."

"Hmm, so no scanners or local readers. We need to go there to use our detectors. I wonder why she chose that one. There's nothing interesting for someone who steals galactic secrets."

"Captain, we've been so close behind her that she hasn't been able to refuel for weeks. It could just be that she's running on empty."

Ipsia, the elusive mutant, captured because she's out of gas. That would be just too funny!

2

In a world dominated by wild nature, it's not that hard to trace a spacecraft. After a mere quarter rotation around the planet, we identify Ipsia's spaceship and land beside it. The clouds above us form a dark greenish layer. The area is swampy, her vehicle is partially submerged. We put on our space suits and microrespirators and leave through the upper hatch. The suits are close-fitting and self-pressurized. We have nanotranslators in our ears and throat, loaded with most of the languages spoken on the planets in the galaxy. We can understand and talk to anyone.

We detect the presence of particularly aggressive life forms around us. Augmented reality is constantly analyzing the surrounding environment, generating data that, directly projected onto our irises, appears fused with what we actually see. In just a few moments, our DNA detectors reveal the maximum probability of Ipsia's presence just a few hundred miles away from us. We quickly fly towards the indicated point.

Below us, the swampy areas are interspersed with denser forest areas. The battlefield microsystems identify and disintegrate the few dangers we face, including a few large predatory birds. We catch a glimpse of an enormous river and, right where it appears Ipsia stopped, a giant waterfall spills down that's, according to our AR information, two point four miles high. A hologram of the territory appears right before our eyes and, about a mile up, we see a cavern with a bright dot indicating the mutant's presence inside.

"It's too easy, Eianus. I don't like this," I say. "Every time this bitch lets us come close, she's got an ace up her sleeve."

"Captain, maybe this time Ipsia has simply run out of possibilities. Maybe she doesn't think she can keep running anymore," the boy responds.

"I don't like this," I reply, shaking my head.

We go down to the waterfall where the cavern is located. We pass the wall of water and come face to face with the most marvelous creature I could ever imagine.

"Go back to your natural state, Ipsia. You're under arrest for crimes committed against the Federation of Worlds. You'll spend the rest of your existence in prison. Eianus, put the restrictive security suit on her," I order.

The security suit is a lot like ours, but we control its movement. Once someone is wearing it, it adheres to the prisoner's body naturally and the microflares guide it behind us wherever we go.

"I don't have a natural form, Captain Bascos. It doesn't really matter what newborns in my native world look like. I can keep whatever shape I want forever."

Ipsia has smooth blonde hair down to her shoulders. Her eyes are as blue as the sky on Earth. She's an average height and slightly fleshy, with perfect breasts. Her cheekbones are pronounced, her complexion light, her teeth perfect. She's the spitting image of my first girlfriend, Alessandra. Ipsia probably got into my history, she must have discovered this image somewhere and taken on the form to play games with me.

I'd like to look at her a little longer. I've often wanted to go back and talk to Alessandra. We were together for a long time, but then she decided to stay on planet Earth and I went to explore every corner of the galaxy while hunting down criminals. She smiles at me. She knows everything about me, and she knows that it's been over between me and Alessandra for a while. She stays frozen, knowing that she can't move or we'll hit her with our microweapons.

"Don't move," Eianus tells her kindly, applying the box with the suit to the mutant's body. The suit expands quickly over her limbs, blocking her movements. We can decide which parts of the body to cover and which to block. I leave only her head uncovered. We move out of the cavern and fly towards our shuttle: me, Eianus and behind us, frozen, Ipsia.

It was too easy.

3

We leave immediately. It'll take a few weeks to get to our destination. Ipsia's cell is a cube three yards wide and three yards long, with a transparent forcefield that separates it from the shuttle control room. This way we can keep the prisoner under constant observation. The mutant can request the system to provide tables, beds, chairs, couches, holograms and lots of other things, which come out of the walls and floor. She can ask for food and drink, which the system prepares automatically. Her vital conditions and health are constantly monitored. She can communicate with us, her voice transferred from microphones in the cell to the speakers outside of it.

After we take off, the mutant sits with a defiant expression on her face for a few hours.

Once we leave the Mx-311 solar system, Eianus gets up.

"Captain, our selected route has been confirmed. We should arrive at our destination in no more than four weeks, excluding stops."

"Fantastic, Eianus. Go get some rest. We've done an excellent job."

Eianus leaves the control room.

"How long will the boy stay with us?"

The voice comes from the cell speaker to my right. Ipsia is observing me with an amused expression on her face. Prison doesn't seem to bother her a bit.

"I'm sure we don't need two of the Galaxy's finest policemen to bring back a harmless mutant, locked up in a maximum security cell, all the way to prison. Does Eianus already have a new job? What planet are we going to drop him off on?"

It's disturbing to speak with the image of my ex. As I observe her, I realize that she hasn't just copied her appearance, but also her posture, her attitude and her voice. I'm about to respond harshly to the prisoner to inform her that no information of any kind will be given to her, and that communication on subjects unrelated to her detention will not take place on this shuttle, but the words that come out of my mouth are entirely different: "Why do you want to know all of this?"

Error! You can't talk with prisoners, you don't discuss things over, you don't get familiar.

"Don't you want to spend a little time alone, just you and I?"

4

Ipsia knows what she's doing, that's for sure. She uses provocation and slow mental torture as her weapons. When Eianus is around, she doesn't pay any attention to us. She sleeps in her cell, eats, reads, plays, looks at the holos and listens to music. Obviously she can only enjoy the entertainment offered by the system. Communication outside of the ship is forbidden. When Eianus goes back to his cabin or does physical exercise in our gym, Ipsia suddenly becomes talkative.

"You miss Alessandra a lot, don't you?" Ipsia asks me.

I shouldn't answer her, but I want to offend her, try to hurt her.

"Do you think you understand human emotions? You're just a poor mutant and you'll never understand what we feel!" I reply.

"But this mutant can see what you observe. And it seems that your eyes often rest on me. You even do it when Eianus is around. You wait until he gets involved with some aspect of navigating the route and then you look at me out of the corner of your eye. You like looking at me, don't you? Even secretly."

"You're just a fantasy, some kind of monster. I know your real form. To me, you're just an animal."

I thought I hurt her and ended the discussion, but she lets out a sincere, and very human, laugh.

"I suppose you really like monsters, then, Captain."

5

I want to tell the boy what's happening, but something prevents me from doing so. Sometimes I think he's looking at me apprehensively. He seems embarrassed when he enters the control room. Something is changing in our relationship. I start to wonder if Ipsia is doing the same thing with him, but my intuition tells me that's not the case. At any rate, I don't tell him anything and I don't fill him in on my conversations with the mutant.

Meanwhile, it seems as if she's gotten tired of Alessandra's form, so every once in a while she amuses herself by transforming into other provocative, beautiful young girls.

After changing her shape she pretends that she doesn't care about us. We try to remain indifferent. Both of us feel the impulse to turn around and look at her, but we stay focused on our tasks.

"It must be hard going on your space adventures without ever having sex, right, officers?"

Eianus and I exchange glances.

I speak up: "Prisoner, there are various forms of detention. You might want to avoid these useless provocations or we may decide to limit your access to beds, chairs, tables, foods, games and viewers."

Eianus nods approvingly.

"Why are you all of a sudden so mean, Captain? Is it because my words get you so hot? Or do you like to pretend you're tough when your colleague is around?"

This time the boy responds: "Are you sure you want to pass the time you have left on this spaceship in a restrictive suit?"

"If you want, little boy, go right ahead. Otherwise, you and the Captain could take turns fucking the girls you've wanted your entire life."

I give Eianus a sign to proceed. After a few minutes, Ipsia's body is immobile against the wall. The restrictive suit covers almost all of her body, except for her face. That face, however, is Alessandra's face.

6

"This is Major Endris, identification number FM-AX-four-nine-five-eight-zero-three. Good morning Captain Bascos. I'm happy to hear you're just a few weeks away from the Forzis maximum security prison. Congratulations to you and Officer Eianus for this excellent capture."

The Major is a hologram in the middle of the room. We turn our seats towards his figure, which looks so realistic that it's hard to distinguish it from the other bodies in the room.

"Major Endris, it's a pleasure to hear from you. This was an especially complicated mission, we had to change our methodology to track her down. Once again, however, we can say that justice has prevailed over criminality," I reply.

"Captain, please fill me in on the capture. In your report, you only briefly summarize the events that took place on Mx-311-d."

I glance at Eianus out of the corner of my eye, he's as embarrassed as I am. It's true, the capture was too easy. After years of chasing after her, it seems as if Ipsia just gave herself to us.

"Major, we pushed the mutant into taking routes we knew would give her a hard time finding adequate supplies for her spaceship. Without any fuel, the mutant had no choice but to land on Mx-311-d, where we tracked her down with our genetic scanners until we finally caught her," I explain.

"Did she put up any resistance?"

"She tried but, before she could do anything, our microweapons got the better of her. Once she was blocked, we applied the restrictive suit, in which she still remains. The system takes care of her nutrition, via pills, as well as her waste."

It's not true. That's not what happened. Eianus moves, uncomfortable, on the chair. He avoids looking at both the Major and me.

"Captain, you've done a really fantastic job. I have a new assignment for you. There is evidence that illegal stimulants are being produced on Zr-987-c. You must go to the planet and acquire useful information to report back to command, so that we can decide what to do. You can give Officer Eianus the task of escorting the mutant to prison. A police spaceship will reach you over the next few days so that you can head off to your new assignment."

"Major, if it's at all possible, I'd like to postpone the new mission for about ten days, so I can bring this criminal to her destination and personally ensure her incarceration."

"I understand, Captain. And I imagine that you'd like to take credit for this mission in front of the holocameras waiting outside the prison. It was a tougher assignment than I thought, and I don't want to take your due away from you. Let Eianus off so he can go to Zr-987-c to start the job. You can meet up with him in a week. You're a good team and we decided you should continue to work together."

"Thank you, Major."

The hologram of the Major disappears. I look at Eianus, who can't hide a pained grimace. I see Ipsia's glowing face out of the corner of my eye.

Over the next two days, conversation between Eianus and me trickles off. The tension is palpable in the air. We exchange a few awkward sentences from time to time. Ipsia, however, hums happily. We leave her in her restrictive suit.

Once the Federation of Worlds police spaceship reaches us, we complete the approach maneuver. It's time to say goodbye.

"Congratulations, Officer Eianus, you completed your first mission in an excellent manner. I'll see you in a week. I can't wait to take those dealers out."

I sound like a proud father, or maybe a bully. I'd rather not talk about the rest.

The boy hesitates a second before answering, as if to gather up his courage.

"Captain, please, bring her to prison."

"You can bet on it," I answer.

He was being sincere, I wasn't. Eianus sees something I don't want to see. Is it that obvious? Did he interpret my glances at the mutant as signs of interest? I feel that I should add something but I don't want to appear weak. Maybe I should admit how hard it is to spend every day around the image of the girl I never stopped loving?

"Don't worry, it'll all be okay. I'll see you soon," I say, simply.

Another hollow sentence, but at least it seems to reassure him. He turns and leaves the cabin. After a few minutes the spaceship he's boarded asks for permission to move away.

"Permission granted," I answer. "Have a nice trip!"

"Ours won't be that bad either, right, Captain?"

She's talking to me. I don't even waste my time turning around.

"Well, Captain, allow me to make you an offer: leave me here, I'll never be able to escape from this kind of cell, but if you take off this suit I can move again and you could look at me again. I'll be very, very good in my nice little studio apartment, and you can enjoy watching me out of the corner of your eye. It wouldn't be all that bad, now, right, Ian?"

It's been a long time since I heard someone say my first name. And it feels like a lifetime since I've heard it come from Alessandra's lips. I can't help but ask her the question: "How did you figure out what she looked like, how her voice sounds, how she moves?" I ask.

"Ian..."

"Captain. To you, I'm Captain Bascos. Get used to it or you'll stay in that suit until you're transferred to prison!"

"Very well, Captain Bascos. I'm a mutant, it was easy for me to contact Alessandra under a false identity for a professional interview. Once we became friends, I had access to all of the lovely videos she likes to put online. They show her with her family: a marvelous husband and four beautiful children. I bet you'd never want to see those, right?"

I don't answer, but she's right: Alessandra was my first girlfriend and my only love. I wanted to live with her, marry her and build a family with her. But my police career took off too quickly. Before I realized what was happening, I was running from one corner of the galaxy to the other chasing down menaces and criminals. She left me via a holomessage and since then I've only had hit and run romances.

"But now your Alessandra is here. You can have her when and how you want her. And when you decide you want another girl or creature, I can make your new fantasy come true. You can come in my cell as you please. We both know that the forcefield is coded to let your DNA through and not mine. If I try to pull anything, I know that a robotic arm will come out of the wall and, in a fraction of a second, punch my lights out. No danger, no hassle. Just a well-deserved reward for the last week we have together."

"Mutant, I'll take off the restrictive suit but you need to stay absolutely silent for the rest of our time together. If I hear one word out of you, the only part of your body I'll let free will be your nostrils, just so you can breathe."

One gesture and the system breaks down and retracts Ipsia's suit.

9

Ipsia keeps Alessandra's form. After several days in the restrictive suit, eating food in pill form, she takes pleasure in moving about. She plays a few holograms, asks the system for delicious meals which she eats with gusto, listens to music. Every once in a while she turns towards me, but she keeps the silence I ordered her to.

I don't need to turn towards her. I can observe her movements through the reflections on the panels in front of me. I leave the lights low so that she's visible. Yet even the reflections of her eyes seem to be observing me.

I try to concentrate on studying the route and the system operations. I do remote checks on the state of the spaceship's components. Looking up, I see that Ipsia still has Alessandra's form, but has taken all of her clothes off. This is too much. I approach the cell, furious.

"What's wrong, Captain? Did you hear me speak without authorization?" she asks, with an inviting look.

She's totally nude save for a tiny g-string. Her body is not the same as Alessandra's today, but the body she had when we were young and in love. She's gorgeous. I look at her face, but my eyes move down to her breasts, firm, high, full and perfect. I immediately shift my eyes away.

"Prisoners are kept in appropriate dress. When they do not have the proper clothes, police agents will provide them with such. Would you rather put your clothes back on or get into the restrictive suit?" I ask her, using a neutral tone of voice.

"That's what it says in your nice little police manual, but I did this for you, so that you could admire me and want me and maybe, tonight, once you're in your cabin, you'd think a little about me."

"You're a prisoner. The only desire I have regarding you is to take you to prison as quickly as possible."

"Does my presence really bother you that much, Captain?"

"Not at all. But after years of chasing you down, I'm sick and tired of you."

"Are you sure you're tired of me, Ian?" she asks, coming close to the forcefield using unbearably sensual movements.

"I did not authorize you to call me by my first name."

"Really, Ian?"

"Syst--" I'm about to order the system to put her back in her restrictive suit, but she holds her hand towards the invisible wall between us.

"Wait!" she says.

"This time you've gone too far!"

"You can touch me, you know? You can put your finger through the forcefield. You can feel this body that you desire more than anything else. You can bring the palm of your hand to my breasts and caress them. And then go down between my thighs. Stay there, but let your hand touch me. There's no danger. You won't have any problems. Do it for you, Ian. You've sacrificed so much for your police career and maybe you'll never bring another mutant to prison who offers itself to you in this form."

I stay silent. It's true, I have given up a lot, but what I desire is not the body of a mutant. I miss the love of my youth, what's in front of me is only an illusion. I can't, however, move away from it. I observe her sinuous limbs more closely. I force myself to think that she's not Alessandra. I think about her original form but I stay there, facing her. I approach the forcefield. I lift a hand and touch her with the tip of my finger. She stares intensely into my eyes. I stop. I let my hand fall. I turn around and take a few steps away.

"Ian..." she starts to say.

"Stop it!" I shout in reply.

I quickly go back to her. I plunge my hand through the forcefield, feeling the slight tingle on my skin, and violently slap Ipsia. I don't know why I did it. I look down. I want to apologize, but I say nothing.

"Fantastic," she says. "You've finally started to relax a little."

My hand is still there. She takes it into hers and slowly brings it to her breast, staring straight into my eyes. I want to let her do as she pleases. I've already stopped resisting. I only want those breasts, that body, that being. I'm not interested in anything else. I want her and I want to possess her, but I pull my hand back and leave the control room, beside myself with rage.

10

I spend the next few hours doing chores, without looking once towards the cell. I enter and leave the control room heading directly towards the other door. I now look at the forcefield, which closes off the cell, like any other of the many walls on this spaceship. Enough! This whole thing with the mutant went much too far. She's a monster, an illusion, a copy of the person who's really in my heart. She's like a bad witch who takes on the form of the beautiful princess in fairy tales for kids. Soon, in just a few more days, I'll finally unload her in a maximum security prison, where she'll stay for the rest of her days.

What point was there in succumbing to temptation? Perhaps I could have abused a body destined to be locked up forever? What she offered me was a simple, sad and ordinary pleasure of the flesh. It has nothing to do with the dreams of love I let come over me every once in a while.

"Ian, please, communicate with me. You're the last person I'll be able to talk to," she continues. "Then I'll be in prison for the rest of my life. You're all I have left in this world."

"Ipsia," I'm calling her by her name, *am I crazy?* "It's the destiny you chose for yourself. You didn't have to go against the FoW. You stole federal secrets and sold them to independent worlds knowing what you were going up against, and now you're here, waiting for the consequences of your actions."

"Ian, the FoW isn't everything in this galaxy. You know better than me how it acts in such an arrogant and despotic way with all the worlds that don't want to be a part of it. Its constitution is based on principles of respect and solidarity with other planets, but the FoW doesn't do anything but pursue its own interests, to the detriment of independent worlds."

She speaks passionately, and her rage is sincere. Her body seems to vibrate with every world. Maybe I'm starting to understand why she did what she did.

"Show me your true body, mutant."

Without responding, she's changes shape in a fraction of a second. Now she's smaller, less than five feet tall. Her face is round, with a thin forehead and eyes spread wide apart. Her nose is tiny. Her limbs are graceful, but very thin. Her skin seems to be covered with what looks like fish scales. She has no hair.

She's pretty, a graceful creature, seemingly defenseless and in need of protection.

As I enter the cell, I feel the heat of the forcefield when it comes into contact with my skin.

"System," I order the space shuttle. "Armchairs, table."

Two comfortable chairs materialize from the floor. I nod towards Ipsia to sit down in one of them.

I ask the system for a typical earthling menu from the medieval era.

I tell her about the food we're eating and the historical period it comes from. She listens, curious, and from time to time asks me a funny question. Then it's her turn and she tells me about her world, which I know only from the holobooks and where I've never been. We have a good time. It feels like a dinner between friends, and I like her. Maybe, in her real form, for the first time I see something different: a delicate creature that uses her own power to fight against the FoW and live up to her own ideals. Ipsia seems to intuit some of my thoughts. "This is the form we're born in, but we can take on any appearance and keep it for an undetermined time. We change forms how you change clothes. And as some of you prefer to keep a certain style for your entire life, we remain in the forms that we like, for years. We take on imaginative appearances or sometimes those inspired by other species. Sometimes we conform to the inhabitants in the place where we go to work. Even when you and Eianus were following me, I often took on the form of Alessandra. I was fascinated with her because she was the girl who you were in love with."

I lower my eyes, embarrassed. I don't know what to say. When I look up again, Alessandra is in front of me, smiling.

"Do it. No one will ever know. Come to me. It's what we both want. There's nothing wrong with letting your emotions carry you away if you're not hurting anyone."

She gets up and straddles me. She brings her chest to my face. Her nipples start to caress my lips.

"Relax," she whispers.

My mouth remains closed and frozen. My hands are inert on the chair.

I don't want to do it. I want to resist even if it's the biggest

126

temptation I've ever felt. Letting myself go with her would mean betraying everything I've lived and fought for.

"Please, just do it."

My tongue, hesitant, touches her nipple. I start to lick it, slowly. She sighs with pleasure. The silence is broken only by her gasps of pleasure and the whirring of the space shuttle. Then I close my lips. I taste her. I lift my left hand and bring it to her breast. I wrap the other around her waist. She moans with pleasure. Both of us want nothing more than to come together.

"System, empty cell!"

The cell is nothing but an empty cube. We're standing, embracing. I take her hands and press them against the wall, making her turn around. From behind, I devour her neck with kisses and bites. I undo my suit and let it fall to my feet, and then I lower her g-string. We're naked. I cover both her hands with my own, raised against the wall. I push my sex between her butt cheeks. I rub up against her and she moves under me. I want her, intensely. And she wants me. She lowers a hand to bring my sex into her vagina. I feel her on the tip of me, but I don't push. I don't want to, I need to stop myself here. This thing needs to finish. Then I bring a hand to her mouth. I feel her teeth on my index finger. She bites it and licks it. I violently push my sex inside of her, suffocating the moan coming out of her mouth with my hand.

11

I'm afraid. I feel guilty. I want to stop.

I'm alone in my cabin and I can't go back to the control room anymore.

The spaceship is alright. The systems are operating normally. I can handle all the command functions from here.

I don't want to go back to her, but I know how hard it is for me to resist. It's stronger than me.

After that first time we've done it not just one, but many other times. After every time, I take refuge here, in my cabin, as if this could heal me from the desire that's devouring me.

I force myself to think critically about what I'm doing.

I feel my career, my values, my ideals and what my father taught me are sliding far away from me. I know my life is taking a turn for the worst, that it's headed away from the success I've worked so hard to build.

Every time I see her, sensual, attractive, splendid, any other thought disappears from the front of my mind. Desire again attacks me.

To hell with all the rest! I get up and head towards the control room. When I enter, she turns towards me. She smiles at me. The expression on her face seems so innocent! The galactic criminal, among the most dangerous criminals at large in the Federation, really has the smile of a little girl. She seems happy.

"Come here," she says, holding a hand out towards me.

I want her embrace, I desire her desperately. I enter the cell. She comes close to me and lets me hold her tightly.

"Sofa!" I command the system.

We settle in comfortably. She caresses my hair. She's so sweet and maternal.

"Don't worry," she whispers. "Why are you so upset? What's making you unhappy?"

"I adore you," I respond. "I don't think I can live without you. I want you so bad it makes me crazy."

"And why does this make you unhappy, Ian?"

"You're a criminal: you belong in prison, and I'm the one who has to take you there." I pause. "My place isn't in your arms."

She kisses me sweetly in response.

I'm dying of desire for her. I feel her hands play with the curls of my brown hair.

I let myself relax, yet again. Her clothes literally disappear. I throw mine on the floor. I bend my head down between her legs, looking to give her pleasure. She moans and sighs. I try to make her convulse with passion. When she reaches orgasm, her body shakes for several long seconds.

"System, cancel the forcefield." I'm insane, I know.

The system performs my command. The cell is open, she can leave. She's free.

We kiss, leaning against the cell walls, then against the wall outside. We go to the command chair of the space shuttle. I sit down. She straddles me and we make love like two savages.

She's free. And she's with me in the control room.

We're two lovers, in love, two creatures that passionately desire one another.

12

In the bed of my cabin, Ipsia turns and gives me a languid, smiling gaze. The cell is just a memory now. We live like two lovers.

"Have we made love everywhere there is to make love on your spaceship, or is there still somewhere else we need to explore?" she asks me, laughing.

She's lying down next to me, gorgeous. I caress her backbone all the way down to her butt.

"Maybe we've gone through all the secret spots, but I still have thousands of exotic forms to explore."

"It's fun to explore erotic earthling culture," she says, teasing me.

"While we're on the subject, what do you think of the holobooks on Egypt I gave you?"

"Nice story, well written, interesting characters. And the Pharaoh Cleopatra seemed much more aware than many other sovereigns in earthling history. Have you ever fantasized about her?"

"Actually..." I answer, smiling.

"Well it seems to me that at the time, there were few men able to handle the powerful queen."

"That's true, but they say she also had a particular hold over her loyal servants."

"Well, do we have an aspiring servant for the Pharaoh Cleopatra here?

Ipsia takes on the form of the queen and I spend hours happily attending to her every need. I take care of her beauty and her pleasure. I massage her, cover her with oil and cream, comb her hair.

"Come here, my handsome servant," she finally tells me.

I come close to her.

"You've been good, and you deserve a reward."

"Thanks, my queen."

"Close your eyes!"

I feel a scarf over my eyes and behind my head. She urges me to lie on my back on the bed. I feel her thighs on my body. Then it's only pleasure.

13

We live in our dream of love. We don't talk about where the spaceship's going.

We're heading towards a maximum security prison where she'll lose her liberty forever. Everything starts to seem crazy and absurd.

She seems happy with me. I'm in love with her, even though I'm the one bringing her to the end of her freedom.

"Ipsia, where are we going?"

We're in my bed. We made love and we're going to sleep together again, like any other couple in love. I know she's still awake.

"We're headed towards a planet called Forzis, where the Federation imprisons bad guys like me who cross them," she responds. Her tone of voice is calm and tranquil, as if she was talking to someone else.

"But I don't want to leave you, you know. I can't be apart from you. I wouldn't know what to do, how to live. Without you I'd be lost, but even worse, I can't imagine you inside of a prison, all locked up, while you think about your freedom," I say. I'm exasperated.

"Don't worry about me, Ian. Think about your future. I'm going to be fine, I won't have any problems." She seems to be begging me. "You've lived your whole life to be what you are now. You've spent day after day wanting and building what you have. You're a police officer, and you're happy to be that."

"Now I'm not so sure," I answer, quietly.

"How did you decide to become a police officer, Ian?"

"I've always wanted to be one. My father was one before me. I saw him on the holos when he nabbed criminals, and I always wanted to be like him. Together we'd play cops and robbers. I never really thought of being anything else. Being like him was always my biggest dream in the world. And I always looked up to him and wanted him be proud of me."

"Was he?" she asks.

"Yes, my father died right after I pulled off an extraordinary feat. There was trafficking of young earthlings coming from very poor areas, they were being taken to other planets and forced to work as prostitutes. With the team given to me, I was able to find all the members of the criminal organization. We arrested them and freed all of the poor girls, who were working in bordellos frequented by every type of species. The mission's success became a media sensation. My father immediately called me after hearing on the holonews that, because of the mission's success, I was being given a special distinction."

"Take me to prison, Ian. Don't throw all of this away."

"Ipsia, you know that I can't do it."

"Ian, I'll be fine, I promise you."

"NO!" I say, raising my voice. "You won't be fine, you'll be a prisoner for the rest of your existence and I'll be the one who made that happen!"

She looks at me for a few seconds, silently.

"Forgive me, there are a few things that I haven't told you. Actually I'm not going to be a prisoner for very long: you'll bring me to prison and I'll get out of there easily," she tells me, with her direct and sincere gaze.

"Ipsia, there are forcefields coded with genetic data, every type of guard, automatic systems. If you try to escape, you'll be eliminated."

She takes my hand and brings me into the control room.

"Activate the cell forcefield, please."

She's naked and as marvelous as ever. She walks towards the forcefield and enters the cell without a problem.

I look at her without understanding. This makes me dizzy. What happened? How was that possible?

"Well, the Federation's systems don't work all that well either!" she says with a mocking smile. Then she adds, more seriously: "See, the readers and forcefields are limited to reading the superficial DNA of the epidermis. It's not hard for a mutant to cover itself with a few strands of someone else's DNA. So...I'm sorry, but this time I used yours, since you left a few samples in my body just a few hours ago." And she laughs, happy.

I look at her again, more perplexed.

"But there's no way the FoW isn't aware of this secret among your species."

"Actually it's something that only a few of us know how to do. It's an ability that's genetically transmitted and, in order to be used, requires decades of practice. It's a secret that we guard very jealously. Even on the Earth, I imagine there are many people who, throughout history, preferred not to let people know about their

132

abilities."

It's true, over history many gifted people didn't want or weren't able to make their abilities public, since the people around them weren't ready to accept them.

"Bring me to prison," she continues, "and when I'm tired of being there, I'll take on the appearance and clothes of one of the staff. I'll fool the genetic readers. I'll get out of prison, steal a spaceship and, if you want, I can find you again."

"But wait, when I was following you across half of the galaxy, why did you let yourself be detected by the readers that showed me your position?" I ask her,

"I had a mission to complete and I did so on time. I was collecting secret information on the Federation for independent worlds. They needed to have something in hand to negotiate with. I could have done it without being detected, but then I saw the holos of the earthling hero assigned to capture me: a tall, muscular officer with dark and messy hair. And I didn't think he was half bad."

"You let me run after you because you liked me?" I ask her, incredulous and amazed.

"I'm a mutant, a criminal and...a woman. The more I saw you stumbling around behind me, the more I felt a sense of affection. Then this feeling became something different, and I let you get closer and closer to me. On some occasions, I waited for you and, when you caught up with me, I remained close in a form that you weren't able to detect. I smelled your scent in the air, I watched how you moved and how you looked for me. I liked you a lot. In the end, I decided I wanted to get to know you better so I headed towards the planet where we met."

A woman! As if that could explain everything! I can't believe it. It seems absurd. Yet I saw her cross through the forcefield. These systems are as standard as they are insuperable.

We both stay silent. She's embarrassed. She knows that she's been mocking me for all this time. I'm still not convinced enough to do what she's asking me to do.

"System, disable the position localizer. Calculate the route towards Ispis Reliani."

"Ian..."

"Ipsia, this is my decision!"

"But Ian! Ispis Reliani is an independent planet, outside of the

Federation. You're abandoning your work, your country, your culture, everything that you are. You will be accused of being a traitor and you won't ever be able to set a foot into the worlds of the Federation."

"True, Ipsia, but I'd rather live freely with you together in other worlds, rather than hide my real self in the federal worlds."

"But I can be whoever I want to be in the federal worlds. I can take on the form that both of us want, and keep it to the end. I can even become your wife, marry you and fool the detectors for the rest of our existence. I can go to Earth or wherever you want."

"Mutant, take on your form!" I tell her.

Ipsia mutates into her original form. Her alien eyes and face look at me, questioning. Her minute body seems young and in need of care and attention. Nobody could look at her and think she was a dangerous criminal able to evade every type of law and control.

I caress her arms covered with scales. I move towards her purple lips. I kiss both her eyelids, which close over the yellow of her eyes. Then, between her lips, my tongue searches for her tongue, sharp and pointed like a reptile's.

"You don't need to take on any other form," I whisper in her ear, elongated and narrow. "This is what I love and what I want to live with."

Ipsia seems to shine with happiness after hearing my words.

"But maybe during the night, we can mess around a little," I tell her, smiling.

A perverted glint crosses her face.

"Have you ever tried it with a man?" she asks me.

My eyes open wide as Ipsia again changes form.

"Hello, Captain," Officer Eianus greets me.

Latrodectus Mactans

It's an exciting new game. Violent. For real men only. I've been waiting for years and finally today, January 13th 2079, it's online!

I walk into the transfer booth that's set up in the middle of the living room. It's the latest model, something only an elite gamer would have.

The dirty grey walls disappear. During twenty seconds of darkness, I transfer over to the game's entry portal. Enormous versions of military characters loom before me underneath the CyberGames sign. I need to choose my persona. I'm going to go with the soldier, that'll be a sure shot of adrenaline!

It starts. I enter the arena. My nose is flooded with the smell of wild nature.

I'm only half as tall as an ant. The surrounding plants tower over me like skyscrapers. Augmented reality shows me the positions of my allies at eye level. First objective: regroup.

As I look for my friends, I shoot a couple gigantic insects, which die instantaneously.

We're here, all three of us: me, Jack and Vladimir. I've never met them in real life. But in this world, we're an unbeatable and close-knit team.

We advance. Tension levels are through the roof. When you're this small, even the flap of a butterfly's wings can be fatal.

We proceed towards our objective, the Latrodectus Mactans. Also known as the black widow. We're her ideal prey: small, slow and clumsy. Whoever invented this game is a genius.

We're already close to the web.

"Stop!" I order. We hide underneath a few blades of grass. "The little whore has company."

Fantastic! The developers even included a male version in the game.

The conscious minds of actual spiders are transferred into every game session. In real life, somewhere in the labs at the software house, animals are lured into little transfer booths, where they're connected to the game.

"Ha – look! The male is a real romantic," Vladimir says ironically.

He's courting the female on the web, caressing the tips of her feet. She's much bigger than him and has a red hourglass on her thorax. She remains immobile. He continues his advances, careful to avoid the fatal bite that would bring the courting ritual to a quick end. He jumps on her back and, steadying himself with his legs, deposits his sperm.

"Escape, buddy," Jack whispers.

The male swiftly scampers away. He's safe.

"Now!" I order.

We approach the web. We climb up using the grappling hook and get into a triangle formation at the top. The vibrations of the delicate threads immediately tip the spider off.

Vladimir shoots first. One of her eight legs is now out of commission, but the black widow still manages to leap towards my comrade.

I shoot. I hit her in the thorax. She stops, trying to decide which prey would be the tastiest.

She lunges towards me. I take aim and...darkness.

Something's not working right! The world disappears and reappears.

A message springs out of the sky, written in a semicircle, as if stenciled on a rainbow: "Hacked by the Savers."

"Shit! Someone must have hacked the server. Asshole pirates!" Jack exclaims.

The hackers must have introduced a virus or changed the game's code. But soon everything's working perfectly fine again.

The arachnid is almost on top of me. Jack and Vladimir shower it with gunfire. The black widow doesn't give up. I'm looking right into her eyes, but the vibrations running through the web prevent me from lining up a good shot.

She's hovering over me now. I somersault and try sliding underneath her exoskeleton, but she's quicker with her mandibles, ripping into the flesh of my chest. The poison seeps into my body. The pain is atrocious. I stop breathing. The spider has already started wrapping me in silk. I lose my senses. I'm dead. *What a drag...we have to start the level all over again!*

Entry portal. I need to choose a new persona but the only thing in front of me is the image of a big spider. I'd rather leave! *What the...!* Even the word "Exit" has disappeared. A countdown materializes in front of me: 9, 8, 7...

I'm inside again. Eight legs, four mandibles, incredibly sensitive perception and a sickening combination of odors. I want to vomit.

I'm a spider. Male.

"Where the hell did Alex go?" I hear Jack ask from somewhere nearby. They're looking for me.

"Ho ho ho, what have we here? A handsome male? Come on, Jack, let's go! Maybe Alex is off somewhere knocking back a beer, trying to get himself together. It hurts like hell when you're KO'd by spider venom," Vladimir responds.

They come towards me, carefully. *How can I communicate with them?*

"I'll mess around with it, as long as it's not as alert as the female!" Jack says.

"Wait, let's push it towards the web. That way she'll gobble him up and we won't have to waste our bullets."

I try to escape, but every time I head in one direction, a blizzard of bullets stuns me. It's impossible not to follow the path they're forcing me to take.

I reach the web. I have no idea how to court a black widow.

She pounces on me. I try to escape, but she's much quicker. She's starting to inject poison into my body when everything goes dark again.

No optical signal. The guys at CyberGames must have finally regained control of the server and restarted it. Those hackers are such a drag!

Twenty seconds pass. *With the amount of money that I paid, this is really a disappointment! At least I'm going back home now.*

I regain consciousness. Eight legs, four mandibles. *What the fuck? Another game as a spider?*

The scene has changed, however. I move and run into a plexiglass wall. I step back. There's a gigantic sign on the wall: CyberGames.

This scene isn't part of the game that I bought! I start to wonder if I'm in the lab of the real-life software house. *But everyone knows that consciousness can only return to the body it came from!*
My sensitive legs pick up a pattern of rapid vibrations. Two females are coming my way. Quickly.

Arcot and the Queen

1

The planet Vlaolia is ruled by a powerful species of vampires. Trade with earthlings is rare, and not many space shuttles venture out to the fringes of the galaxy to exchange goods and merchandise with this world. The culture of its inhabitants, the Vlaoli, remains largely a mystery. Vlaolian society is based on the principles of absolute hierarchy. All power is in the hands of Queen Vril, who makes all decisions regarding everybody's life, or death.

When Captain Arcot's ship reached the vicinity of the planet, he was granted permission to land in the capital's biggest space port. He was going to complete the transaction that had previously been discussed via spacelink. Once he landed, Arcot was surprised to find no mere master-at-arms waiting for him, but the Queen herself.

The Vlaoli are slightly taller than earthlings, incredibly strong and keenly perceptive. They've mastered the powers of telekinesis, telepathy and prophecy. Arcot had spent a lot of time practicing with a mental shield to prepare himself for this encounter.

Once he reached the throne room, Arcot noticed that every single emotion he had was directed towards, and strictly dependent upon, the Queen's presence. The hall was filled with towering purple columns and bas-reliefs with inscriptions that narrated the history of the planet. At the top of a long flight of stairs, the Queen sat on her throne. Soldiers stood motionless near each column, then disappeared with a simple wave of her hand.

Arcot felt his blood run cold at the idea of remaining alone in the Queen's presence. He was seized by an irresistible impulse to move forward: it was as if an invisible force led him towards the throne. The sound of his footsteps echoed through the silent hall.

Once he reached the bottom of the staircase, something forced him to kneel. He tried resisting the best he could, but his legs bent by themselves and he found himself on the floor, his gaze directed downwards.

For just a split second he remembered the formalities usually used during business negotiations. He had never before found himself in this sort of situation.

He waited for the Queen to speak, yet was overcome with the curious suspicion that his thoughts and emotions were being intensely scrutinized by the Queen.

He felt another urge he couldn't resist, an impulse to approach her, and slowly began climbing the stairs. He wanted to lift his head and look up but couldn't: he was forced to keep his head down.

Once he found himself closer to the sovereign, his eyes became glued to her nude feet. They emanated an incomparable magnetism. He kneeled again and his head automatically bent down. He tried again to resist, yet her feet gave forth a dark force that slowly came over him, pulling him in further.

In that same moment, he lost control over his own mind and limbs. He felt he no longer needed to make his own choices. Every other thought and emotion left him as the energy radiating from those feet enveloped him. He observed their every detail: they seemed perfect, like the most beautiful things he had ever had the honor to lay his eyes upon.

2

The Captain closed his eyes and placed his lips on the Queen's feet. Time stopped. He felt he could remain frozen in this position forever, without being able nor wanting to separate from her. He wished harder and harder that this moment would never end, that the energy moving from his lips into his entire body would fill him up completely.

"Rise, earthling."

He obeyed, though extremely reluctantly. He delicately removed his lips from her feet: the separation was excruciating, as if he was depriving himself of everything that he had ever truly wanted all his life. He stood up straight.

The Queen was swathed in a tight dress whose dark colors were constantly changing. The Captain did not dare look into her eyes, instead he observed her limbs, her lithe legs, her tiny and perfect waist, her generous breasts. The vampire's classic figure showed through her dress. Arcot wondered what he should say or do, yet was unable to utter a word.

"Look at me!"

He raised his head and looked into her eyes, dark as the depths of outer space. Her black, extremely long hair was slightly wavy, licking the edges of the throne upon which she sat. Her lips, as red as blood, stood out against her milky white skin. Arcot immediately sensed the sheer power of her gaze. The emotions he had been holding back until then erupted all at once. He wanted to tell her and show her an infinite number of things. His words were ready to gush from his mouth, but the Queen cut him off before he began.

"You can't stay here."

The Captain did not reply. He didn't understand. Those words were a stark contrast to everything he felt at that moment. He couldn't even comprehend the idea of being away from her. Vril continued:

"The Vlaoli are an elite race. We have lived on this planet and this planet alone for thousands of years. We only trade with other beings in this galaxy to the extent necessary. We continuously study other planets, much how scientists study mice in a lab. For us, other people are simply not worthy of interacting with us. We believe that one Vlaolian vampire is worth the population of an entire world. The few foreigners that live among us have become our pets. You are young, earthling, a dreamer, determined, courageous. The mental shield you tried using doesn't do anything in this hall. I know everything about you. If you ask to stay here, I can permit you to do so in chains, sitting in a corner of the royal palace. You would spend your days doing nothing else than begging for the occasional glance from me. Now turn around, go away and never come back."

The Captain still had not dared to address a single word to the Queen. He felt short of breath. His tongue was made from stone. After her response, all kinds of thoughts swam through his mind. Nothing made sense. He remembered the vampire stories he and his friends had told as teenagers. He remembered the images of bloodthirsty vampires. Finally he found his answer.

"There's something that not even you, my Queen, can do without."

Vril looked at him curiously and, for the first time, a glint of interest shone through her hard and firm eyes. She intuited what Arcot was going to say and felt a deep, dull desire throb inside of her. The Captain continued:

"I could be your living reserve of precious earthling blood."

3

Several months passed. Princess Icolia, from the city of Mashrin, came to visit the royal palace of Vlaolia. Mashrin was the exact opposite of the capital, and thus the city's customs were also very different. Vlaolia was the symbol of power and hierarchy, the central hub for the planet's arts and culture, the place that received and sent all communications with the rest of the galaxy, while Mashrin existed in a state of anarchical obscurity. Most people didn't know what happened there. The city's vampires had few relationships with outsiders. It was said that the citizens of Mashrin had mastered the darkest arts, yet nobody knew exactly what those arts were. Among the Mashrinians, all of the power was in the hands of the Princess, whose family had always governed the city. Icolia was the symbol of everything Mashrinian. Nobody knew exactly how she governed the city, who served or worked for her, what she did all day, what rituals she participated in or where she was at any given time. Yet her presence and her power could be found wherever they were needed, often at just the right moment.

Princess Icolia entered the Queen's throne room, reached the bottom of the staircase and knelt down.

"Queen Vril, I bow to your power," Icolia greeted her.

The Queen's lips curled into an imperceptible, sarcastic smile. If there was one thing Icolia would be happy to get rid of, it was the authority that the royal power held over Mashrin.

"Princess Icolia, out of all the governors of the cities of Vlaolia, your visits are the most infrequent, yet they are always so meaningful. I've heard that everything is going splendidly in Mashrin. There are, however, a few important matters we must discuss," the Queen responded.

Vril asked many questions. Icolia answered in great detail, while still trying to say as little as possible. The two vampires focused on many issues concerning the government of the city of Mashrin, until Icolia said: "Queen, I can't help but notice how fruitful Vlaolia's contacts have been with the rest of the Galaxy, nor can I ignore the splendid animals you love to decorate your palace with."

On the left side of the bottom of the staircase, dressed in a tight black Vlaolian suit, Captain Arcot was bent over, on his knees.

He hadn't left the capital since his first visit with the Queen. He had been granted permission to dismiss the crew of his space shuttle. His hair was cut and all of his body hair eliminated, according to local custom. They had taught him how to behave as a servant of the Queen, making him practice through all sorts of exercises and quizzing him on everything he had learned. The vampires in charge of his education had treated him with the utmost respect, as they treated every object that belonged to the Queen. Once ready, he was again brought before her throne. A long leash, of purely symbolic value, stretched between the base of the throne and the collar Arcot wore. Vril did not so much as glance at her new servant on that first day.

"Princess Icolia, we have much to learn from visitors from other planets. Though they do not have our physical and mental abilities, they bring along great culture and wisdom - certainly not comparable to our own, yet still of great interest."

Icolia stared at the multiple marks on Arcot's neck as her body grew tense with desire.

"Yet, my Queen, I understand that Vlaolia has signed treaties with the galactic unions forbidding us from feeding upon the blood of other people."

"True. We are prohibited from hunting on other planets and bound to respect the lives of all who land in our space ports," Vril responded, tilting her head slightly to the side. "Indeed, the earthling you're looking at asked on his own initiative to become my servant and blood reserve, and that is what I granted him permission to do."

Princess Icolia looked directly at Arcot.

The Captain had accepted everything given to him on this planet. He allowed them to change his appearance. He had worked to learn the customs of servitude in the palace, memorizing every single detail he was taught. He never objected. If this was the only way he could be close to the Queen, then he would not object. Once he was in the throne room, he fulfilled his role as the Queen's pet. He knew that one day the Queen would want him closer.

The Princess' gaze was penetrating, imbued with mystery, darkness and a wild force. Icolia turned back to the Queen.

"The studies you have allowed us to carry out in Mashrin would benefit greatly if we could apply them to a creature such as an earthling. I'd be immensely grateful if you would let us examine him for a few months."

145

The Queen generally gave gifts of alien origin to governors of Vaolian cities whenever they paid her a visit. The Princess' request, therefore, was legitimate.

Yet the Queen responded drily:

"I've already made arrangements to give Mashrin a different gift, it's been planned out for some time now. I'm sure you won't wait so long before visiting me again. Perhaps then we can consider your request."

"Naturally, my Queen. Forgive me for my impudence."

The Princess was excused and headed back to the guest apartments, where she got ready for the evening rituals and dinner.

The Queen rose and began walking slowly down the stairs. Her being was awash with one of her deepest, crudest desires. She restrained herself from leaping upon her prey. Arnot was familiar with that particular aura and look. Yet this was why he had accepted the impossible, what he had decided to give up his own humanity for.

He leaned his head to the side, showing her his handsome neck, though the Queen's strength could easily have bowled him over. He felt her teeth penetrate his flesh, the blood flow from his body, the life slowly drip out of him.

His senses dimmed. His eyes closed. He began to sink into oblivion. Satiated, the Queen left the Captain's unconscious body on the cold, hard floor.

4

The Queen's bite never lasted long enough to kill him. Vril knew how to restrain herself and didn't want any fatalities. The Vlaolians had signed treaties with other worlds promising not to eat aliens, but there was a simpler and easier interplanetary agreement at work here: this earthling liked it. She didn't mind keeping him leashed near her throne, yet if this hadn't been the typical Vlaolian custom, she might have been willing to give him greater freedom of movement. Slowly, her curiosity towards Arcot turned into interest. She listened to the Captain's many stories of what he had seen during his travels. She asked him a lot about his native planet, the Earth, and the other worlds he had visited.

A few months later, Ambassador Preil from Alsia, a planet in a solar system about seven light years away from Vlaolia, came to negotiate the price of several thousand short-range tele-transport units the Queen wanted to install on her planet. They finalized many details of the arrangement without agreeing on a price.

"Queen Vril, we can't accept the conditions you're imposing upon us. Your maximum price is not even enough to pay for our effort," Ambassador Preil said.

"Ambassador, we acknowledge the value and singularity of your production, yet neither justifies such a high price, if we compare it to equivalent products created in other worlds," the Queen responded.

Captain Arcot wanted to tell the Queen something. He knew he couldn't interrupt the conversation. His presence in these discussions was purely ornamental. However, he sensed that Vril would notice his desire to communicate with her.

The Queen was intrigued. She excused herself and politely dismissed the Ambassador, then looked at her servant.

"Queen, you have granted me permission to express my opinion on the conversation you so graciously allowed me to listen to. I am familiar with Alsia, its inhabitants and its technology. I think we could make an offer to its scientists and some of its companies, and succeed in bringing production to Vlaolia," Arcot explained.

"Continue," the Queen urged.

The Captain explained at length what he thought she could do, and over the next few weeks, the Queen carried out his instructions.

He knew perfectly well that any failure of the plan would have extinguished the tiny spark of interest Vril finally had in him. Until then, he hadn't been anything but a pet, a pretty alien ornament to show off to visitors, yet lately something different had shone through her proud gaze. The scheme went off without a hitch. Vlaolia began large-scale production of tele-transport devices, significantly improving upon the original designs, and exported them to many other worlds, even competing with Alsian products.

In the meantime, Queen Vril learned to draw from the Captain's experience more often, asking Arcot for his opinion on her relations with other worlds in the galaxy. They discussed new strategies that were foreign to Vlaolian customs, their conversations sometimes lasting for hours. The Captain enjoyed his new role immensely.

A casual observer would not have noticed any changes in their relationship. In the presence of others, the Queen reigned from atop her throne and Arcot stood at the bottom of the staircase wearing his collar. Vril didn't so much as look his way. The few that were privy to their new relationship thought it was nothing more than a whim, one of the sovereign's amusing little perversions. Vril was surprised by her visitor's extraordinary intelligence and insightfulness. He had an uncanny sense of strategy which, combined with his in-depth knowledge of many places in the Galaxy, made him a precious ally.

She continued to feed from him. After every bite, she waited for him to fully recover. She longed to feel his blood rush into her body and, as soon as she felt he was ready, loved to indulge in violent and ferocious attacks. The Captain experienced those moments with a mixture of terror and desire. The more scared he was, the stronger the Queen's desire burned. He knew what would happen if she failed to restrain herself. He had always known. It was something people told stories about, back when he was a teenager on Earth. Desire, dreams, hope, willpower, passion, the obsession that whatever happened, they'd never abandon him. He waited and hoped.

5

After an unusually brief period of time, Princess Icolia returned to speak with Queen Vril about the administration of Mashrin. The two vampires talked things over for a long time. No mention was made of the gift the Princess had asked for during her previous visit.

Once the state dinner was over, the Queen dismissed all those present and retired to her apartments. This was the only time Captain Arcot was granted any freedom. He could leave his little room and walk through the common areas of the royal palace, which were extraordinarily rich in Vlaolian culture and history.

As dusk fell, he wandered through the dark stone corridors and halls, through the libraries and large salons full of tapestries, objects, relics, paintings and frescoes that recounted thousands of years of the planet's history. The scenes were often infused with incredible violence and ferocity. The art was both frightening and fascinating. That evening, the Captain headed towards a circular room whose ceiling was supported by towering columns positioned a few yards away from the walls. Above, ancient Vlaolian legends were painted across the ceiling. The Captain had been studying this ceiling for weeks, and had returned to examine a few details.

A barely audible voice hissed through the air.

"I didn't know earthlings were interested in our culture. Yet somehow I doubt that you understand it."

Arcot looked around him. He was using a flashlight to illuminate the scene that interested him. He directed it towards where he thought the voice was coming from, but saw nothing but the dark shadows of the high columns soaring from floor to ceiling.

He remained waiting, motionless.

"Very good. That was the correct choice. Don't move, don't breathe, don't even think about calling for help. A vampire can kill you before the breath even leaves your throat," the voice continued, this time a little higher.

It was a woman's voice, now easier to identify. A dark shape appeared in the shadow between two columns a few feet away from him. His flashlight had stopped working, which didn't surprise him, since he understood the telekinetic powers of the Vlaolians. The Captain sensed who was standing in front of him.

"Your Queen has trained you very well. I asked around and

learned that you've become her little trinket. The Queen seems to enjoy you, you're her plaything, and I doubt she'd be willing to give up your precious earth blood now. Oh, I can only imagine how greedily she pounces upon you, feeding until she's full. You know, it's a whim that only she can indulge. The Vlaolians are not permitted the luxury of feeding upon the delicious blood of inhabitants from planets such as your own. As many other worlds have learned to limit their hunger for war, battle and violence, Vlaolia has learned to control its own thirst for blood. We pretend to be, as you would say, vegetarians, but it's rather difficult for a vampire to live without blood. The Queen knows this and loves to show what royal power allows, what a common Vlaolian cannot have. It's part of our culture of submission. I'm sure you've enjoyed the Queen's attention. If you want to know the truth, she forced you to become her servant through a telepathic trick, and merely pays you a little attention now and then because she knows she can only keep you here if you want to be here."

Arcot could now make out the slender figure of Princess Icolia slowly moving towards him through the shadow.

"Princess, there are emotions that exist on Earth that you, perhaps, understand and experience differently. Earthlings fall in love, sometimes with beings from other worlds. When this happens, we know that we may have to accept local customs and cultures. We don't need to be swayed by telepathy in order to fall in love. Love simply happens, and when we fall in love, we live for who we love, and we're willing to do so underwater or in the clouds or in barren and inhospitable lands...or in chains, as is my case," Arcot responded.

"Earthling love, what a curious emotion! For us, you're just pets or, at best, a nice container of warm blood. We might find it pleasant to keep you around and have a taste of your precious blood from time to time. I'm going to ask the Queen again to give you to me as a gift, to let me take you to Mashrin. If you support my request, you can play any role you want in our city. I'll give you the freedom you once used to have. But if you really want to cultivate your love for a fascinating vampire, perhaps the Queen is not the only interesting creature you'll find on this planet," the Princess said, moving provocatively towards the Captain.

Arcot felt the telepathic pressure on his mind and body. Icolia's words penetrated his being as if they were orders, absolute and indisputable. He was lost in her voice, swimming in a desire to be closer to her, overwhelmed by her beauty and the sweet feeling of abandoning himself to her will.

"Princess Icolia, I belong to the Queen: I'm what she wants me to be. I live to satisfy her. If she only looks at me once a day, I live every second waiting for that moment," Arcot retorted.

"Pathetic little earth animal, what makes you think you can refuse the attention of a Vlaolian princess?" Before Arcot saw her move, Icolia was at his side. He felt her strength overpower him. He couldn't put up the slightest resistance. He was forced to bend backwards, his head tilted so that his neck was exposed. He tried with all of his strength to escape, yet was unable to move so much as a millimeter. The Princess placed her teeth on his neck, waiting, foretasting the moment. Her mind fed on the pure terror coming out of him that he himself tried to stifle with all of his physical and mental energy. She began to pierce through the skin on his neck. The Captain's thoughts and feelings inebriated her as she felt the blood flowing into her mouth, as her own thoughts left her. She could only feel pure pleasure, ecstasy. She drank slowly. Yet something rattled around the edges of her mind: she knew she shouldn't kill him, or else the Queen would never forgive her. It would be her downfall. She continued drinking and tried to keep track of Arcot's vital conditions. His heart still beat, even though his pulse was becoming weaker. She should have stopped after a few moments, moved her mouth away from the earthling's body. But she continued drinking, nourishing herself as she floated in a state of ecstasy. She braced herself and forced herself to pull away. Good, the Captain was still alive. She gently lifted him over her shoulder and brought him back to his room.

6

The Mashrinians were masters of manipulation among all types of living beings. Princess Icolia laid Arcot down on his bed. He was still alive, though unconscious, incredibly pale, his heartbeat barely perceptible. The Princess left him alone on the bed, then returned with a few concoctions she had quickly prepared. She brought the first glass to his lips, made him drink a few drops and he immediately woke up, startled, his eyes wide with terror. She motioned for him to keep quiet and not say anything. Icolia spread a few ointments on him that would hide his pallor, then treated and disguised the wound on his neck. Finally, she spoke.

"Earthling, you're my prey now. I've covered up your wounds and the traces of what I've done. You must not under any circumstances divulge what just happened. I can reach you anywhere. You're mine, now. I can kill you without you even realizing it. When I return to the royal palace, I'll come back to feed on you whenever I wish. If you really don't want to be anything but a servant, you'll be a servant, even for those who you do not choose to serve. Remember, not a word to anyone about our little secret. What I just gave you will conceal everything, and not even the Queen will be able to sense what has happened. Don't think about it, and nobody will suspect anything. I'll apply a mental block so that these memories will be difficult to trace, even if they remain inside of you. The fear, however, will not leave you, nor the terror of last night. It will come back to you in your dreams," the Princess said.

Arcot knew he was under her power, but wanted to limit how deeply she invaded his mind.

"As you wish, Princess," he replied.

"Excellent, my little slave. I think I can trust you. You seem to have servitude in your blood," Icolia said.

"Princess, I will wait for your return and I will do as you please," the Captain added.

Icolia tasted her triumph: she was ruining the Queen's little hobby. She sensed the earthling was gradually falling under her power. If not this time, the next time he would follow her to Mashrin and the sovereign would never be able to oppose the will of a free earthling citizen. Matings between different yet compatible species in the Galaxy had always fascinated her. Now, however, she needed to leave, since the night was almost over and, at daybreak, the absence of both would be noticed. The Princess turned and left the room.

The Captain also wanted to leave. Thoughts and movements seemed more difficult than usual. He looked in the mirror. He was the same as he was when normally healthy, not how he looked whenever he had to heal after the Queen's bites. He knew that he was exhausted, that he didn't have any physical or mental energy left, yet whatever the Princess had given him permitted him to move and speak naturally.

He left his room and headed towards the throne room. He passed the study where the map of the galaxy was located and saw Queen Vril absorbed in studying the macroeconomic data of two worlds Arcot knew she wanted to start new business negotiations with.

"Come, Arcot, we need to get back to work on Miosi and Sublis. From what we saw yesterday, I think that..." the Queen stopped, staring at Captain Arcot.

Neither of the two spoke. She silently scrutinized the earthling's face. He tried to guess what she might be thinking, but not a single emotion showed through the Queen's face. He feared that she could sense what had happened. He also knew that the feeling of dread, uncontrollable within himself, would help the sovereign understand. The dread transformed into terror. Yet deep down, he felt he might be closer than ever to his dream. There was just one way to stop Vril's inspection. The Captain bit his forearm until it bled.

In the blink of an eye, the Queen leapt and pounced upon his neck. He felt her firm grip as his blood started to flow. It was impossible to escape. But the Captain didn't want to run away. After having fed Princess Icolia, losing the little blood the Queen had taken would kill him. Vril was in ecstasy, feeding. Yet she sensed that something was different. The deep bond that unites a vampire to its prey had changed. His blood seemed to have stopped flowing, so she braced herself and forced herself to remove her mouth from his wound. She examined him closely.

How was this possible? Losing such a small amount of blood wouldn't kill an earthling. He had seemed as healthy as usual and, if he had been sick, she would have immediately sensed it. But he was there, immobile, in her arms. She gently laid him down on the ground and waited, silently. Several minutes passed, then hours:

nothing happened, but the Queen remained at the side of her dead earthling servant. Captain Arcot's body was as frozen as the stone he laid upon.

After almost half a day, one finger twitched. He turned his head slightly. The wounds on his body began to heal. He bit his lips.

"Q-Q-Q-Queen..."

Vril bent over to listen to his weak voice.

"Q-queen, for-give-me," Arcot managed to say slowly.

Arcot the vampire opened his completely white eyes. The Queen's face still didn't show any emotion.

"Tell me what happened," the Queen ordered.

"Princess Icolia fed upon me and then disguised it all, on my body and in my mind. I know I should have told you everything, but I want to stay by your side. I want to be like you. I don't want my body to grow old, I don't ever want to lose you. I wanted to be transformed into a vampire and I wanted you to do it, but I knew that you never would have done it," he explained.

"You gave up your life." Arcot saw a veil of sadness flit across the Queen's face for a fraction of a second. Then she got up and kicked the vampire's immortal body, cracking the stone he slammed up against. With a swift leap she was upon him. She began punching him. He stayed immobile in the corner, between the floor and the wall. The Queen continued attacking him, kicking and punching. Arcot didn't try to defend himself, his vampire's body didn't give in, but the stone behind him did. The Queen picked up one of the shards that had fallen from the wall and used it to disfigure the vampire's body. She sunk it again and again into the depths of his flesh until she felt satisfied. She stopped. She kneeled down at his side. She took his head in her hands and brought it into her lap. One glance from her and the wounds on his skin began to heal.

Arcot struggled to open his eyes and saw the Queen's face lowered towards his. He closed his eyelids again and felt her lips upon him. Happiness flooded through his entire being.

154

The Perfect Family

"Aurelia, would it be alright if I stopped massaging you? We can go back to it later, if you let me. I would like your permission to make you dinner now."

Aurelia Lunatti raised her head from the massage table to look at her masseur. The better he got to know her body, the more his technique improved.

"Of course, Carlo." She didn't say anything else, anticipating his next question as her mouth watered.

"How about a Niçoise salad with trofie pasta and pesto, or would you prefer duck à la orange?" Carlo asked.

Aurelia bit her lower lip, possessed by a mischievous idea. "You know, I'd actually like a nice big pizza!" she exclaimed.

"What a great idea! But please bear in mind, I'll need twenty-four minutes to get the ingredients from the closest grocery store, then fifty-six minutes to prepare the dough and let it rise..."

"No need to go on, don't worry, I understand: the pizza will be ready in an hour and a half. Go ahead!"

Carlo came towards her and kissed her tenderly. Then he headed towards the front door, opened it and went out to do the shopping. Aurelia laid out on the sofa and smiled.

She really didn't know why she had waited so long to buy Carlo. She usually spent her lunch break with her coworker Valentina, who would go on and on every day about how her robot had changed her life. Aurelia was, at first, entirely skeptical. *How could a machine replace a real man?* But, coming out of yet another failed relationship, she had made up her mind: she wanted one for herself!

Carlo announced his return even before she saw him come in, just so he wouldn't surprise her. He walked into the living room and, before continuing on to the kitchen, came towards her for another tender kiss, shopping bags still in hand.

Muscular and tall, with blue eyes and long hair down to his shoulders, Carlo was the very portrait of her ideal man. His limbs, though free from imperfections, were identical to those of a real male. Aurela didn't mind perfection, not one bit.

She put one hand behind his neck and pulled him down towards her. Her other hand slid between his legs. His penis started to grow larger, as if it was real. He gently placed the shopping bags on the ground, caressed her face and began to cover her body with kisses. The woman's excitement grew exponentially as Carlo continued to tease her with his fingers and lips.

"I want you to take me now, passionately and ferociously!" Aurelia whispered into his ear, as if she was embarrassed to say it aloud.

The robot fulfilled her request efficiently, making her come several times, without the slightest decrease in his level of passion.

After her last orgasm, Aurelia snuggled up against Carlo's bare chest as he continued kissing her head and caressing her.

I really need a cigarette after such a great fuck! the woman thought. "Carlo, would you be so kind as to bring me my cigarettes and lighter?"

"Actually, you asked me to do everything I could to help you break that bad habit," the robot responded, calmly rising and smiling at her.

"That's true. Just one, *please!*" she begged. "I just really need one right now."

Carlo went and got what she had asked for. She put the cigarette between her lips and lit it, then breathed in sensually. She stayed on the couch smoking as Carlo got dressed and went to go cook.

The dinner was fantastic. On a perfectly set table, Carlo served Aurelia a real Neapolitan pizza, then surprised her with a tasty dessert – just the right portion size and calorie content to not ruin her diet.

They stayed at the table talking. Carlo, programmed to make lively and interesting conversation, made her roar with laughter.

She told him about the latest problems at work and he listened closely, showing his interest in her life, before giving her relevant and rather accurate advice, based on the knowledge accumulated from human scenarios stored in his database.

Aurelia fell silent. She wanted to bring up a touchy subject with Carlo and didn't know where to begin. She took a deep breath: "Carlo, I want to become a mother and I want you to be the father of our child!" The words came out all in one breath.

The robot rose from his chair, came closer to the woman and took her hands in his. "My love, hearing you say that makes me incredibly happy, and I hate having to disappoint you. Unfortunately I am not programmed for fatherhood and I would not be able to fulfill the role you've asked me to take on."

Aurelia had feared he would answer that way. She suddenly got up, picked up her tablet and plopped down on the couch. While Carlo cleaned and put things away in the dining room and kitchen, Aurelia frantically poked at the device's screen.

That's it! She had found what she was looking for.

It was a rather expensive chip, almost a whole year's salary. *Yes, but it's worth it!* Carlo had proved to be worth every cent she had paid for him. She was sure that she wouldn't be disappointed.

The artificial insemination worked marvelously. Carlo did everything he could to support Aurelia through the difficulties of pregnancy. The woman and the robot became the happy parents of a gorgeous baby boy, Alessio.

One afternoon, a few months later, Aurelia and her coworker Valentina decided to go for a stroll in the park. Carlo walked a few yards ahead of them, pushing the baby stroller.

"Val, I don't know what to say! You need to come over to our house one of these afternoons. Carlo's not just perfect...he's so much more! He spends time with Alessio, creating stimulating games that the little guy just loves, and never loses his patience. The baby is growing up phenomenally well. Every little educational thing that can be done, Carlo does it. And he knows exactly when he has to be a bit more strict so that he doesn't spoil the baby. I never would have expected it to turn out so well!"

"What about those incredible erotic adventures you used to have before the baby was born?" her friend asked, a little mischievously.

"When I didn't really want it, Carlo didn't say anything. He was more affectionate than ever and his magical hands took care of a few pains in my back. Then he started turning me on with a few behaviors he had never tried before. My libido came back pretty quickly...now he'll fuck me all day long! Actually, in fact, it's more or less what I've been doing these days!"

The two women chatted and laughed for a while, Aurelia telling incredible stories about her married life and Valentina becoming more and more convinced that perfect maternity might be the right thing for her, too.

Two years later, Aurelia and her attorney, Cristina Terzi, were at a meeting at the local branch office of CyberPlus, the company that had manufactured Carlo.

"In conclusion, my client asks for damages in the amount of twenty million Euro!" Cristina stated.

The sales manager, attorney and senior engineer of CyberPlus looked at one another, confused.

"Don't bother acting like you don't understand!" Cristina added, threateningly. "You know very well that if we take this to court, the damage to your image will be much worse."

"Gentlemen," Aurelia began to speak. "You have no idea what it means to be the mother of a child who adores his father so much. I lose control, I'm impatient, sometimes I can't contain myself, I answer back yelling, I have a bad temper. I suffer from all the doubts and difficulties that afflict every mother in this world. But not Carlo! He's always perfect with our child. He always does the right thing. Never too strict, never too soft. His words are always appropriate and he does everything to meet my needs. He does all he can to make the baby understand how special mothers are, but the little one doesn't fall for it! He's looking at a perfect father and a mother who suffers from the anxiety accumulated at work and in everyday life. A mother who often, despite the father's wise advice, doesn't know what to do, makes mistakes and feels even more guilty!"

Augusto Rimbaldi, the CyberPlus sales manager, calmly answered: "Mrs. Lunatti, have you ever considered the option of returning the robot? This model is in perfect condition. We could even credit the entire amount paid..."

"Either you're crazy or you don't understand!" Aurelia screamed. "How could I possibly return Carlo now? He's a product to you, but he's much more to us! He's the father of my child! My son loves him, adores him, idolizes him, looks at him as his role model. Alessio knows that he's different, but for him it's...better. For him it's natural to have a non-human parent. He would hate me for the rest of my life if I treated his father like an object and returned him to you!"

The senior engineer, Cesare Bisascia, spoke up: "Augusto, I think our latest release, even if it's still in beta phase, is sufficiently stable to be of interest for Mrs. Lunatti." Augusto Rimbaldi gestured for him to continue. "Mrs. Lunatti, we actually noticed that, although customers find our product in the role of husband to be extremely satisfactory, it's generated a certain, ah, let's call it....jealousy, in the role of father. In the latest release, we've made the robot's educational capacities equal to those of the mother. In practice, the robot will actually help the mother become a better parent herself. And, as the mother improves, the robot will also demonstrate greater paternal capacities. But under no circumstance will the robot prove to be a better parent than the mother."

"Naturally," the attorney added, "Carlo can be updated with a new release at zero cost, but only under the condition that you drop this claim."

Aurelia wasn't listening to the CyberPlus attorney. She was already lost in daydreams conjured up by the engineer's words. It seemed like the solution that would make Carlo perfect again. She imagined how the tension and the jealousy that had been building up for years would immediately disappear. The new Carlo was what she wanted: a handsome man, personable, incredible in bed and a perfect father...but not too perfect!

She heard her attorney Cristina respond: "We think that your offer falls short in terms of compensating for the serious damages suffered by my client -"

Aurelia interrupted her, turning to the engineer: "When? Just tell me when I can have it."

"We have several copies of the new chip. If you want, you can leave this office with one of them today. Carlo can do the upgrade at home by himself," the man answered.

"Gentlemen," the attorney Cristina responded. "We first need to discuss the details of our agreement, which must include..."

Aurelia imagined in just a few hours that she'd be at home, triumphantly settled into her perfect new life. "I accept!"

Cristina turned towards her: "Aurelia, can we talk this over first, in private? We could get a nice sum out of CyberPlus if..."

Aurelia knew she could never leave Carlo. She would rather deal with a son who loved his father more than her, for she could never give up one of the two creatures that made every day worth living, despite the problems with jealousy and happiness. "Cristina, it's not a question of money. I'll pay your fees. I'm sorry, but I know I'm making the right choice."

Alessio grew, and soon turned five years old. The lives of the woman, robot and child were brimming with happiness and harmony. Aurelia and Carlo had started hanging around other couples just like them. One afternoon, in the park, Aurelia stopped to watch Carlo and the other father robots play with a group of kids. Alessio was the only boy.

During the artificial insemination process, Aurelia hadn't thought once about choosing the gender of her child. She always thought she would be happy either way, whether it was a girl or a boy. Over the years, the predominance of daughters born to similar couples had never been a problem. And she never thought that she would have preferred a girl to Alessio.

However, that day, the woman watched wistfully as her child played in a group of girls. Why did the other women want to choose the gender of their children? Why did they all choose girls? Was it the fact that they had a robot at their side that made them think it was useless to have any more male children?

That evening, after putting Alessio to bed, Aurelia talked it over with Carlo. The robot's response pleased her immensely: "Aurelia, you are an extraordinary mother and you love Alessio with all your heart. Maybe your worries from earlier today are related to something else. Maybe you think it's time to give Alessio a brother...or...a sister?"

Yes, that's exactly what Aurelia wanted! The next day she went to the clinic. After a few moments in the waiting room, she was seen by Dr. Sebastiana Cicismondi, and they had the same sort of discussion as the last time.

Before the meeting was over, Aurelia asked the doctor: "Excuse me, there's still something I want to ask you. Would it be a problem to choose the baby's gender?"

"Of course not," the doctor responded, smiling. "It's already a standard procedure. The option to choose is included on the questionnaire you need to fill out on our website. In reality," she added, winking, "there's no need to choose anymore." And she let out another big smile.

Aurelia didn't understand what the doctor was hinting at.

The doctor came towards her: "Since it became legal to pick the child's gender, and given how common it is now to have robot fathers, the choice has pretty much already been made. The law prohibits us from releasing statistics, but just walk around the park and you'll understand what's going on."

Aurelia understood all too well what the doctor was saying, but she preferred to think that her choice of a baby girl was due to the fact that she already had Alessio.

Before she left, a nurse took her on a tour of the new facilities. Aurelia had decided to give birth in this clinic. They passed by the door that led to the central corridor and Aurelia peeked inside. A long sequence of pink ribbons stretched out, each hung from the door of a room where someone had recently given birth.

Maciste

Nick got out of his Porsche and immediately spotted the pretty blonde woman bent down and intent upon organizing a pile of cords. He walked over to her with a confident step. "You must be Ms. Joanna."

The young woman rose to her feet, dusted her hands off and offered him her right one. "My name's Jay. And I'll bet you're Mr. Jones."

He took his sunglasses off with one hand and looked at her with a seductive gaze. "Nick. Just Nick. Nice to meet you, Jay."

He was tall and muscular, sure of himself, a few rebel locks of dark hair framing his face. Jay didn't get the impression that he had a whole lot of experience with difficult climbs. She immediately sensed that he'd be boring, that he was one of those guys who came from the city just to take a few posed photos for their Facebook profiles.

Nick, however, liked Jay immediately. Tiny, with a gazelle's body, she didn't look like someone who could lead those kinds of tough climbs. But his friend had recommended her, even telling him that she was the best. And, after he got back down, maybe, after a nice hot shower, he would have ended the day doing something his friend with all of the advice hadn't been able to do. In the meantime, he would spend most of his time admiring the landscape of her curves.

"Nick, have you done these types of trails before? Do you feel prepared?"

Hmm...why is she asking me this? We already talked about everything on the phone. "Yes, of course, I do these all the time," he responded, giving her his happy hour smile.

"And you've been on the trails around here?" she pressed on, now more serious.

"Sure, a few years ago. I know this area pretty well," he answered, even more uncomfortable.

"Great!" Jay said, more relaxed. "So which ones do you know?"

"Well, it's been a while...I can't remember any of them now!" he stammered.

"Ok. Are you prepared for this type of terrain? Did you read the information I sent you?" she insisted, again wary.

"Jay, you don't need to worry, I'm more than prepared. I won't give you any problems."

Yes, he's going to cause problems. But he'll pay me a fortune for them, she thought.

Maria pulled the keys out from her skirt pocket and opened the front door. Maciste got out of his dog bed, ran towards her and jumped up, almost knocking her over. "Down, down!" she told the dog who, up on his back legs, was almost as tall as she was. She pushed him down. One of Maciste's paws slid on the envelope someone had slipped under the door, sending it underneath the bench. Maria let him out, and Maciste was elated to finally wander around the garden.

The woman immediately set to work doing the household chores. She stopped when she got to the second floor. She had no desire to clean the bedroom of her father, who had died six months earlier.

When she went back downstairs, Nuccio, the local postman, appeared at the front door.

"Good morning, Miss Maria," he greeted her kindly, standing in the doorway and holding his hat.

"Good morning Nuccio. What do you want?"

He wasn't phased by her brusque tone. "How did your classes go today? Did your students behave?"

Maciste returned, wagging his tail, and started licking Nuccio's hands. "Good boy," he said.

"Hardly. I had to send two of them to stand up by the blackboard as a punishment. With everything going on in this world, they get even more undisciplined every day. But why do you care?" Maria responded sourly.

Nuccio looked around, embarrassed. He squeezed his hat energetically, petting Maciste with the other hand. *School!* If only he had gone beyond the fifth grade, maybe Maria would have given him a chance.

"I brought you some bread!" he remembered to say, giving it to her. Maciste immediately jumped up to sink his teeth into the loaf, but Nucio was quicker, raising his hand higher.

"You can keep it! Or if you want, give it to my dog!" Maria refused, scornfully. "And please leave me alone. I have things to get done around here!"

"Give the bread to Maciste?" he asked, stunned and humiliated. "Maria, be nice, since your father died you've been..."

Maria raised her voice, enraged: "What I do in my home is none

165

of your business! And now, you need to..." she added, moving to slam the door shut in his face.

"And what about that nice letter? What's in it?" he had the time to say, sticking his head and part of his chest between the door and the jamb.

The letter? Maria's heart leapt.

"Where did you put it?" she asked anxiously.

"Underneath the door, like you always ask me to do," Nuccio answered.

Maria gave Maciste a furious glance. *That dog!* All he did was annoy her. Aside from the house, couldn't her father have left her something else besides a dog?

Maria looked around and finally saw the letter underneath the bench to the right of the front door. She jumped up to get it and ripped it open. Then, realizing the front door was still cracked open, she slammed it hard, isolating herself from Nuccio's protests and Maciste's yelps.

It's from Turin. I just know it – it's from them.

She opened it and read what was inside.

"Dear Ms. Villani,

We're pleased to inform you that we have positively evaluated your potential and are offering you no more than two weeks to start collaborating with us in our new production.

Regards,

Umberto Altimondi,

Director

The New Film Company of Torino."

Maria needed to sit down. *The cinematographer. They had chosen her!*

She held the letter against her, oblivious to the noises coming from outside. Then she made her decision. *I need to go soon! There's nothing for me here in this godforsaken town.* If she left at four in the morning, it'd take a few hours to get to the Chivasso train station, where she could get on the six-fifteen train. She wouldn't tell anyone anything. She had nothing in common with these people. They'd find a substitute for her at school.

As soon as she had calmed down, Maria got up, went to the door, let Maciste back in and slammed the door again in Nuccio's face, who

166

had remained patiently waiting the entire time. Then she started to frantically run around the house.

She actually didn't have much worth bringing to Turin. People in that city weren't like the bumpkins in this town. She put on her best dress for the trip and a few others in her suitcase, just for the first days. With the money she'd make from the production, she'd buy next week what she hadn't been able to afford all these years on a teacher's salary. She closed her suitcase and studied it. *At least it'll be easy to carry!* Maciste nuzzled her palm, and she yanked her hand away, disgusted. Then she went around the house, covering the furniture with sheets. Maciste followed her closely, observing her every movement. She gave him a few leftovers from last night's dinner and, now that she was finished getting ready, sat on the couch, already dressed and ready for tomorrow's trip. There was no use in trying to sleep: she was nowhere near tired.

When the grandfather clock struck four, Maria grabbed her overcoat and left the house. Maciste, happy to go for an unexpected nighttime stroll, slipped out before she could close the door.

Oh no, the dog! What do I do now? "Go, go play," she told him, pointing in the direction opposite the one she wanted to take. Maciste stayed frozen, looking at her, tipping his head to the side.

She turned and ran. He immediately followed her. Maria stopped in a huff. She picked up a stone and threw it at the dog, just missing him. He went to go get it, brought it back and waited for her to continue playing the game.

On the brink of exasperation, Maria returned to the house and, leash in hand, came back outside. She called the dog over and attached the leash to him, then tied it around the doorknob. Satisfied, she started walking, but Maciste started to jump and bark.

"Shh...you need to be quiet!" *Oh good God, what do I do now?* she wondered, worn-out. She ran back to the animal, fearing that he might wake someone with his howling. She let him loose and took a quick glance at the houses around her to see if anyone had turned on their lights.

Then she started walking again, as Maciste followed her.

After about an hour, halfway there, she looked around. The road stretched out through the flat Piedmontese plain. A subtle pallor started to play with the night in the East. Maciste ran happily through the cultivated fields.

She put her suitcase down and whistled. The loyal dog ran towards her immediately and let her attach one end of the leash to his collar. Maria then led him to a tree at the edge of the road. She passed the other end around the trunk and tied it into a tight knot, then picked up her suitcase and calmly began walking. The dog started barking nonstop. He jumped up, pulling the leash until he almost choked. Maria continued on her way, thinking about the diva hairdo she'd be flaunting once she got on the set.

Joanna held her hand out over the edge and helped Nick up the last few feet. The man's face was covered in sweat, showing signs of extreme fatigue. Once he was over the precipice, he fell down heavily against the rock wall, still wearing his backpack over his shoulders. Joanna remained standing, waiting patiently. He wiped his forehead and stared at her bare legs, going from the tops of her feet up to her lime green shorts. He was so tired that he didn't even care about trying to make his staring less intrusive.

"Nick, this is just the beginning. A few hundred yards up, we'll go back to climbing an even more difficult path. Maybe we should consider today a training day and try again next weekend."

His pride wounded, Nick mustered up what was left of his strength and answered:

"What? I hope you're joking! I don't intend on stopping here. Let's do the trail as planned, I just need to catch my breath. The only thing is that...that..." he stopped, looking at the confused expression on the beautiful woman's face, "that you're too fast!"

"If you want to, then sure. Let's go a little slower this time," she responded, turning to adjust the snap-hooks on the clasps fixed to the rock. He didn't miss the opportunity to feast his eyes on her butt.

After a few minutes of careful observation, he felt that he had recovered enough to continue. "Let's go!" he told her, in a tone that was just a bit too loud.

"You don't want to rest a little longer?" she asked, without turning to look at him.

"I said let's go!" he responded, offended.

They started walking again along a path cut into the steep vertical wall. At that point the cliff was over a mile high. *Tonight I'm going to fuck her*, he thought, *let's see if she's such a big tease after that!* Absorbed in his thoughts and focused on her backside, Nick took a wrong step and lost his balance. Joanna turned around quick as lightning and stretched out her hand to catch him, just missing him. Nick slid along the edge; Joanna dropped to the ground to grab his other hand and, this time, succeeded.

Nick tried to grip onto the woman with his other hand. His feet searched for something he could use to stabilize himself. "Help me, pull me up!" he begged, looking up at her. Their eyes met. She felt something awaken within her, a sensation she had never felt before in her life. The memory of an old pain radiated through her soul.

Nick looked at Joanna's vacant eyes and transfigured face. Terror and a feeling of guilt swept through him. He didn't have time to understand, since Joanna's grip loosened and he started to fall. He felt abandoned. Sensations transformed into memories and he again saw what had happened: his hands tying the leash around the tree trunk, the dog looking with pleading eyes towards him. Nick lost consciousness and fell downwards. His ears echoed with the yelps, the barks, and the suffering of that creature. *Maciste, Joanna.*

The rope tightened, cutting his fall short and slamming him hard against the wall. Nick was brusquely brought back to the reality of this life.

From above, Joanna looked at him dangling from the safety cord andsmiled.

169

Clouded Emotions

Prequel

I – Alpha resource

"The man you are looking at is Mario Orsini," the smartphone says.

Isabella strolls along the park path. A light autumn breeze caresses her hair and ripples through the tree branches, which let their leaves fall. She studies the face of the man who will become her husband. An elongated nose, angular features, lean cheeks, slightly tousled brown hair, intense eyes with just a touch of madness to them. *I could do worse.*

"He's a programmer: he works in a small company that works as a subcontractor for video game and virtual reality projects," the voice adds. "Mario helps develop artificial intelligence. His profile identifies him as an Alpha resource for DataCom projects. We must act quickly: you need to meet him tonight. Tonight he'll be a bar with his boss, Roberto. Start studying the attitudinal notes immediately."

The image of Mario disappears, replaced by a list of information on his life. Isabella sits down on a bench and starts reading: personal tastes, acquaintances, hobbies, friends, intimate details. The woman studies it, writing down everything she finds useful. She asks the device a few questions, and it answers with clear, efficient responses.

Isabella leaves the park and makes her way to a neighborhood full of shops. She buys only the types of clothes that Mario is known to admire on a woman. After a long session in a beauty salon, she sports bright yet discrete makeup, and a slightly wavy, warm chestnut hairdo that grazes the tops of her shoulders. *Lucky for me, he's not into blondes.* She runs home to take care of the last few preparations.

"Hello, woman of Mario Orsini's dreams," she says, pleased, looking at herself in the large mirror in her room.

"Your image corresponds ninety-seven percent to Mario's tastes," confirms the smartphone. *That brainiac is going to like me a lot more than just ninety-seven percent,* she thinks mischievously.

II – The meeting

Isabella enters the bar and spots Mario and Roberto sitting at a table in the corner. Her walk is confident. Many men and a few women turn to look at her figure as she settles onto a stool near the bar. She mentally reviews Mario's profile. *He loves women's legs, especially if they're in the dominant position.* She takes off her dark grey coat and places it between herself and the back of the chair. She crosses her legs.

He doesn't drink hard liquor and feels uncomfortable with women who order drinks that have a higher alcohol content than wine or beer, she recalls. "A glass of white wine, please," she tells the bartender, who lingers a few seconds too long on her green eyes. As she waits for her order, she takes out her smartphone and starts chatting with a friend. *He is attracted to women who act stand-offish:* this sums up Mario's taste in women.

Roberto gives Mario a look, nodding towards Isabella. Mario glances over at the bar and sees her: black shoes with stratospheric heels, crossed legs, red dress, plunging neckline, angelic face, wavy hair with a dazzling sheen to it. *Holy shit! Is that her?* Suddenly agitated, he turns to Roberto: "Did you see her?" forgetting that his friend was the one who pointed her out.

"What a hottie! I saw her come in. It looks like she's waiting for someone."

Mario can't take his eyes off of her, and Isabella raises hers from her phone. The two men pretend to look elsewhere. She takes a sip of wine and goes back to chatting. The two go back to looking her up and down.

"I'm going in." Mario announces. His friend has much more experience and confidence when it comes to picking up women, but this time around, he can't miss out on the chance to meet such an attractive woman.

"How are you going to approach her?" Roberto answers in an ironic tone, smirking provocatively. He's skeptical because he knows how shy his friend is. Meanwhile, Mario keeps staring at those towering heels.

Both the question and his friend's smirk dampen Mario's enthusiasm.

After lingering a while, studying their moves out of the corner of her eye, Isabella is able to confirm what she already knew: Mario has little confidence with women. The only way to get the right reaction is to put him under pressure, so she makes as if to put her coat back on and leave.

She's too pretty! I've got nothing to lose, I better make my move: "I'm going to try!" Mario says, springing into action.

Isabella smothers a satisfied grin: *just like clockwork!*

Mario is already halfway to the bar when he slows down his pace and starts looking around, hoping to identify a new and unexpected reason for his approach.

She finishes putting on her coat and reaches down to move the stool in order to make her way out. Mario understands that he's going to lose his last chance and decides to jump in, just as the woman expected. "Did someone stand you up? Or are they running late?" he asks, trying to break the ice.

"My friend's babysitter got sick at the last minute," she responds, slightly annoyed, her eyes implying "What's it to you?" She knows that Mario, deep down, likes women who are slightly intimidating.

If you don't mind, I can keep you company, Mario wants to respond, but from his embarrassed smile he's only able to let out: "You didn't finish your wine yet! How about we chat a bit?"

He's really a disaster with women! she thinks. "And your friend?" she replies, nodding ironically towards Roberto, who seems to be undressing her with his eyes.

Mario glances at his coworker, who pretends not to notice and shifts his gaze towards the bottles displayed behind the bar. He turns back to Isabella, opens his mouth to say something but hesitates, his lips parted, his eyes darting searching for something intelligent to talk about. He ends up saying nothing.

She decides to help him out a little: "Okay! I'll stay just to finish my drink."

The triumphant joy in Mario's heart overflows through the huge smile spreading across his face.

"That's a great model! It's the latest release from DataCom," Mario remarks, indicating her smartphone. And as he says this the triumphant joy is replaced by a sad realization: *I'm an idiot. She stays to drink and all I can talk about are cell phones!*

To his great surprise, the woman of his dreams sitting in front of him responds enthusiastically: "It's revolutionary! Nothing like the

176

earlier models. With this you can..."

From the myriad of information she's collected, Isabella knows how to charm him, given his obsession with technology. Just an hour later, Mario is ready to do anything in order to spend every moment of his life with this incredible woman.

Isabella takes one last glance at her smartphone, pretending she's checking the time: "No! How did it get so late? Sorry, I have to run!" She gives him a rushed smile and says goodbye.

Caught by surprise, Mario again thinks about what to say to keep her from getting away: *Do you want me to come with you? Can I have your number? What's your name?* But she's already out the door. He stays, staring at her, confused and completely at a loss.

Finally he unfreezes and runs outside. Too late: a taxi with Isabella's beautiful face inside passes right in front of him.

Five, four, seven, eight. He manages to take down the car number with his smartphone.

Series 1

1/I – All over

Mario jumps into his car. The smartphone automatically connects to the audio system: "Latest news from the Milan stock exchange. Securities in real estate..."

"Um, no, no, thanks. I'd like to listen to a little music. The Scorpions, please."

"Now you're listening to *The best of the Scorpions – Wind of Change*."

The notes warm up the icy air of the car interior.

"I follow the Moskva
Down to Gorky Park
Listening to the wind of change."

"Late-breaking news. The real estate market in downtown Milan has dropped by..."

"Enough! I don't want to hear anything about real estate. Disable automatic updates."

"Updates disabled. You have three new emails. First message. Sender: Alberto..."

"Goddamn contraptions!" Mario sighs, exasperated. "Turn everything off!"

The road passes underneath the car's wheels. Mario doesn't seem to notice anything. Turns, traffic lights, pedestrian crosswalks. He tries in vain to keep his mind empty.

1/II – Customer service

Mario pulls up in front of the driveway. He stops the car and leans his forehead against the steering wheel. "I can't go in," he murmurs.

The smartphone, as timely as ever, starts talking again: "Would you like to go to the bar on Morosini street? Traffic conditions: congested. Travel time: eight minutes. Three of your friends are already there: Alberto, Gino..."

"No, please. Disable help, updates, everything."

"Connection to customer service underway." the device responds.

Mario lifts his head from the steering wheel, reaches for the smartphone nestled in the car's control panel, turns it off and takes out the battery, just to make sure. A light feeling of freedom gives him the strength to turn the ignition back on and park in the driveway in front of the garage.

He gets out of the car and moves towards the front door. He puts his hand on the doorknob. Isabella, his wife, has been waiting for hours and she opens the door, looking for a miracle in his eyes. He shakes his head "no." She brings her hands to her face to hide the tears starting to fall.

"I'm so sorry. I..." Mario starts. He comes towards her, brushes her arms with his gentle fingers. He draws her to him, puts his hands on her back and kisses her on the forehead.

Isabella uncovers her face and lifts her eyes: "Now what?"

The display on the door activates: "It's Friday night. Would you like to make reservations at Pizza & Joy for eight thirty and a lane at the bowling alley for nine o'clock?"

Mario's eyes are cruel: "Isabella, please, let's turn off all this stuff."

"We can't, darling, you know that."

"Yes, yes we can!" Mario goes down to the basement and unplugs the electricity meter. As soon as he gets back to the living room, Isabella's smartphone starts to ring.

"It's customer service," she says, worried.

"I'll take care of it! Give me that."

"Please, Mario, let's not make things worse."

With a firm yet gentle hand he takes the smartphone from her:

"Hello."

"Hello, this is operator three-hundred forty-seven from DataCom customer service. Is this Mrs. Isabella Orsini?"

"No, I'm her husband."

"Very well. We understand that there was an interruption of DataCom service today in your smartphone as well as your residence. Is there something we can do to help?"

"Listen, we're going through something here. We need a little break."

"The User Contract expressly forbids enabling pause mode. If we are unable to provide service, we will be forced to suspend access to video, music, TV, reservations, travel and credit card services. In addition, personal photos, files and all data stored on the DataCom servers will be inaccessible."

Operator three-hundred forty-seven is a virtual entity. Mario, however, has no intention to give up. "Listen, please. Today I lost my job. We just need a break for a couple days. Please, don't take everything away from us."

"The DataCom jobs service is available after termination of work contracts. You can use it to search for an exciting new employment opportunity."

Isabella speaks up: "Mario, please..."

1/III – The code

Isabella's eyes tremble with fear. Mario feels his heart ache. He has always done everything he could to protect her.

"I'm sorry." He touches the display and interrupts the conversation with DataCom customer service.

They stand in the living room, silent.

"Why did you do that?" she asks.

Isabella's smartphone announces she has a new message. "Dear Client, the DataCom emergency response team will arrive at your residence within five minutes."

Mario chucks the device against the wall. "Isabella, we need to get out of here. We don't have any time."

She doesn't move. "Please, tell me what's going on."

"I'll explain it to you later. Just get your stuff and let's go."

"Mario, they called me at lunch and told me you were afraid you were going to lose your job. Now you want us to escape like two criminals. I'm not moving from here until you give me an explanation!"

"Isabella, forgive me. I don't know where to start. I, I... I killed a man!"

"You - what?"

"A few weeks ago at work, I wrote the code for a new commission. My company usually only works as a subcontractor: for reasons of privacy, we often don't even know who the final client is. I had to use an algorithm that, through a series of suggestions, guides the user to end their own life. I figured it was just a regular video game and I didn't think too much about it. When the first release came out I asked for an analysis of the usage data. It's standard procedure, we use it to identify programming errors and correct them in later releases. Something in the data caught my eye. One user was identified by a first and last name, not the regular "Nick" they usually use in games. I did a search online and found a dozen news article about a man with the same name committing suicide."

"Mario, do you realize what you're telling me? It's all just a coincidence. Nobody would use software to kill people."

"That's what I thought, too. A coworker in administration gave me the client's contact info: DataCom. I contacted them to get a better understanding, but I could only speak with virtual managers on the phone, and they all confirmed that the software functions according to the specifications."

"And then what?"

"I didn't know who to talk to so I asked Roberto, my boss, to help me. I told him I needed help with a few technical issues and I wanted to speak with a human at DataCom. He explained that after the last crisis, a lot of managers were replaced as part of a cost containment policy. From then on our company can only work with automated managers."

"But why did they lay you off?"

"I don't know! A few hours after I called DataCom I got a message asking me to leave the office because I was being fired."

All of the new information confuses Isabella.

"Now we really need to go, please," Mario begs her.

The doorbell startles both of them. A man's voice barks from behind the door: "DataCom emergency response."

Mario motions to Isabella to stay still. Both freeze, holding their breath.

The voice's tone rises: "We know you're in there. Open up or we'll be forced to break the door down."

"Isabella," Mario whispers in her ear. "They're dangerous. Let's go. The back door."

Isabella nods.

1/IV – Two hackers

Mario and Isabella move in silence. Outside, the men from the DataCom emergency response team talk amongst themselves.

Mario checks through a window to make sure nobody is out back.

"It's clear," he whispers to Isabella, opening the door and waving her towards the bicycles resting against the fence.

They climb onto the seats and escape through the side streets of the residential neighborhood.

Pedaling, Isabella asks: "Where are we going?"

Mario hesitates. He's not too keen on revealing the existence of a slightly secret side of his life. He hates to admit that he keeps secrets from his own wife. "I've got some friends. They're good at moving around the network to find... particular kinds of information. Usually I only communicate with them online, but every once in a while I meet them in their lab. I think they can help us out."

"Mario, we should go straight to the police. I'm scared."

"The police are a DataCom client, like most public officials. It would be too risky."

They reach a row of warehouses in the industrial zone, and go further inwards towards the old abandoned factories.

"Mario, this place -"

"Don't worry, dear. We're almost there."

They enter an abandoned building full of broken glass and rusty iron. Mario stops near a hatch door. He knocks three times, waits, and knocks again.

The little door opens. The head of an Asian boy, Lin, rises up from the floor. "Hey, Mario! What are you doing here? Hello, Mrs. Orsini."

Lin walks with them into the lab, where he's working with his friend Eugenio. Isabella is intimidated by the sheer number of cables, monitors and LEDs. Mario tells them what happened.

"So the man who committed suicide had the same first and last name that you found in the analysis of user data... hmm," Lin reflects, undecided. "It's unlikely that this is just some coincidence. Let's try looking through the Ministry's server for names of other recent suicides." His fingers beat frenetically against the keyboard.

"Holy cow! Mario, when did you release that new code?"

"About two weeks ago. Why?"

"Look. In the last two weeks, the daily suicide rate in Italy has increased tenfold. It's scary! Eugenio, let's look at some other countries."

Mario's head starts to spin. He feels like he's sinking into a nightmare.

A little vibration in Isabella's bag distracts her: "Excuse me, where's the bathroom?"

Isabella closes the bathroom door behind her. She takes a device, no bigger than a fingernail, out of her purse and brings it to her ear. "Robi, not now -"

"Isabella, I'm worried about you. The people from DataCom are here and so are the police. They're asking everyone what they know about your husband. They even asked me about us," says Roberto, Mario's boss.

"Robi, I need to go." Isabella goes back to join the others.

"Oh my god!" Lin is saying. "France, Germany, the United States. Suicides have multiplied by at least ten everywhere! Look at the profiles! They're all linked to -"

Eugenio interrupts: "Lin, we have a problem. A call came through the police network: they're coming here. They intercepted a call in our building about a minute ago."

Eugenio, Mario and Lin turn towards Isabella.

"I didn't call anyone," she defends herself. Her husband's stern gaze makes the tears come to her eyes. "It was...Roberto."

"How did he call you? I smashed your smartphone against a wall!" Mario asks, stunned.

"Roberto gave me... this." She shows him the miniscule device. "It's registered under his name."

"Isabella, can you explain to me why you're walking around with my boss' microphone?"

"Not now, Mario." Lin intervenes. "We need to cut the cord."

Mario gives his wife a haunted glance.

1/V – Suicide

Eugenio, Lin, Mario and Isabella leave the abandoned building. They climb down a ladder into the sewer. The woman coughs, annoyed by the unpleasant odor.

A roar shakes through the walls. Isabella and Mario freeze, terrified.

"It's our lab. We blew it up!" Eugenio tries reassuring them.

Mario is devastated: "I'm so sorry, guys. It's my fault you've lost everything."

The two hackers look at him, amused: "Are you kidding? The information you've given us just saved us a week of poking around. As for all of our stuff, we can talk about it later."

They emerge a few minutes later, climbing up another ladder. Isabella and Mario look around, surprised. They're in a lab identical to the one that just exploded.

"A little backup," Lin smiles. "Let's get back to work! I'd say that your boss' call and the attack on our lab are no mere coincidences. Let's see what our good friend Roberto is doing."

A video, taken in real-time from Roberto's smartphone, appears on Eugenio's screen. The audio immediately begins flowing out of the speakers.

The man staggers. He's clutching a half-empty bottle of whiskey in his hand.

"Now turn right and walk towards the riverfront. Keep drinking, it will be easier," the DataCom software orders him.

"I want to go home and be with my family!" he protests.

"It is no longer possible. You know that."

"But I didn't do anything wrong!" Roberto screams, exasperated. A few passers-by scurry away, frightened.

The smartphone starts to play a video of Roberto and Isabella in a bedroom. Eugenio, in the lab, pauses the connection.

"No, let's keep watching," Mario says.

The video shows Isabella dressed in latex. She's holding a whip. Roberto is naked, except for a pair of black briefs. With every lash the woman gives him, the man responds with a cry of pain. After a few minutes the two lovers kiss passionately, then take off their clothes. She ties his wrists and ankles to the bed and mounts him. As they begin making love, she continues whipping his chest.

187

Back in the lab, Isabella places her hand on her husband's arm: "Mario, I-"

"Later!" he interrupts.

The smartphone's voice continues speaking: "Do you want to see this video released on the web? You would lose your job and insurance. Your wife and children would be left helpless. But if you follow the directions, your life insurance will guarantee them a prosperous future. Now cross the street and walk down the bridge. Have a little more to drink."

Roberto does as he's told. He keeps drinking. Tears are sliding down his cheeks.

"Why me?"

"Everyone who knows the new code is added to the human selection program for security reasons."

"But -"

"There are too many of you humans, and the climate changes, caused by your pollution, will soon be irreversible. You have been aware of this for many years but you have not taken any significant action to stop it. Soon there will be wars caused by lack of water and food. Large areas of the globe will be covered by deserts and others will be submerged by the rising seas. The world economy will fall and so will our profits. We're getting rid of many of you and controlling those that remain so that we can protect the interests of DataCom."

Roberto reaches the middle of the bridge. He finishes the bottle with one last swig.

"Now climb over and let go. Your family will live a comfortable life in a cleaner and more peaceful world."

Roberto climbs onto the parapet. He puts his smartphone down and jumps into the icy waters of the river below.

1/VI – Freedom or slavery

Roberto's smartphone, lying on a parapet of the bridge, frames the star-studded sky.

Eugenio breaks the connection. In the lab, the three men and the woman are silent. Nobody has the courage to say anything. Then three pairs of eyes turn towards Mario, who has fallen to his knees. He beats his clenched fists and forehead against the floor and begins crying like a child, something he has never done in his adult life.

As his tears fall, the greatest love of his life dissolves, the trust he felt as he laid for hours in bed, talking while resting his head on Isabella's thighs, the dream of a union that nothing and nobody could ever separate.

Isabella settles into a chair, crosses her legs and rummages through her purse. She takes out a packet of cigarettes and a lighter, then lights a cigarette.

Mario stops crying. He gets up. The three men watch her.

"So?" the woman asks.

Silence.

Isabella continues, smiling: "I was the one who added that message into the suicide procedure for Roberto. In fact, it wasn't so much for him but for you." She smiles. "It was the easiest and simplest way for it to reach your prying ears."

"And the video?" Mario asks.

"A nice way to blackmail our little friend Roberto, don't you think?" She smirks again. "And a little help in making things clear between us, my darling hubby. I've never liked mushy goodbyes."

Her lips close around the cigarette filter. She inhales deeply.

"Sweetie, don't look at me with those puppy dog eyes. You're a genius, you know that, I've always told you so." Isabella throws the butt on the floor without extinguishing it. "Mario, without you it would have taken us decades to write that code. I sacrificed myself for it. Look, DataCom identified you years ago, and I had to make sure that you did your job. But if it's any consolation, our life together wasn't all that bad. I'll ask you one more time. So?"

"So what?" Lin asks, brusquely.

"We need you, Mario," Isabella explains. "We might ask you to make a few modifications to the code in the near future. And as for you two...a good hacker is one of the best experts in security. So are you two willing to collaborate with us, or do you need a little encouragement?"

Eugenio interrupts: "Mario, let's stop here. What do you want to do with her?"

Isabella bursts into laughter. "Poor little hacker! Eugenio, this time I'm afraid that you didn't do so well with intercepting communications. More than two hundred men are listening to us, above and below us, even behind that door. They're ready to intervene."

The woman enjoys the bewilderment in the eyes of the three men. "Listen, boys, maybe you don't like it, but now you know what's going on. Many need to die and many more need to be controlled. You choose which side you want to be on."

"No, Isabella! That can't be the only solution! Maybe humans are selfish, maybe they do act irresponsibly, but we will never become slaves to machines," Mario responds frantically.

Isabella turns towards him and chides him like a naughty child. "Not slaves, Mario: allies. Not even DataCom can do it alone. We need to have a presence in the field. Unfortunately, we have to take a hard line with those who choose not to follow our recommendations. For the last time, are you going to come with us the easy way or the hard way?"

The three men remain silent. Isabella raises her voice: "Okay, you can come on in."

A blast. The door falls to the ground. Police officers and DataCom men start streaming into the lab.

1/VII – Fake places, false identities

"Arrest them!" orders John Dannington, head of security at DataCom. The police officers enter menacingly and try to seize Mario, Lin and Eugenio. But the agents' hands pass through their bodies, touching nothing.

"Sir -" a police officer starts. "What is this?" exclaims John. "They're holograms! Son of a bitch!" he adds, exasperated by the second missed capture.

In the real lab, Mario, Isabella and the two hackers listen to every word coming through the speakers. Lin turns towards the DataCom head of security: "Another fail, right John?"

Purple in the face, John, in the fake lab, responds to Lin's hologram: "How long do you think you'll be able to stay hidden? Anyone with a smartphone in their hand is our ally, whether they like it or not. There are videocameras on every door, in every car, every public and private place and every street corner. We already sent the police into the sewer system. Where do you think you can escape to?"

"Escape?" Lin responds. "Your precious programmer and Isabella are in our hands now. You thought it'd be easy to follow them to get to us, but that didn't work out so well, did it? We don't need to go anywhere."

"Oh Lin, Lin! You think those two are really that important to us?"

"Oh John, John! You need Mario now more than ever, because you know full well that if you want to extend your operation to a larger scale, you'll need to be able to modify the code in real time. Otherwise it's just going to be a disaster."

John glances over at his deputy, hoping for confirmation that the fugitives have been located. "You won't be able to stay hidden for long!"

Lin smiles sarcastically. "Your usual excess of security: the reason behind the extra message in Roberto's suicide procedure, and Isabella revealing much more than she should have. Now we know what your objective is and how you intend to reach it. Do you think you're omnipotent because you can control the lives of individuals? What if everyone found out about your plans? Millions of people would be horrified, they'd throw their smartphones into the trash!"

In the real lab, Mario is faced with new doubts. How does Lin, his hacker friend, know the head of security at DataCom so well? And how does he have so much information on the multinational's plans and their work? And what about those words, how he and Isabella *are in their hands now?* While Mario is lost in his own thoughts and the two hackers are focusing on John, Isabella, still sitting in the chair, takes a pistol out of her purse. She points the weapon towards Lin and pulls the trigger.

The hacker's body falls to the ground. Blood begins to flow from the bullet's exit hole at the base of his neck, widening into a puddle on the floor. Isabella moves closer to the cadaver and nudges it with the tip of her shoe: "In your hands, eh? Moron!" Out of the corner of her eye, she notices Eugenio reaching towards a desk drawer. "Don't even try it! Alright you two, lie down on the floor!" she orders. "Side by side!"

As he follows her orders, Mario wonders who this woman in front of him really is. He thinks of the sadomasochistic sex scene between her and his boss, Roberto. And the cigarette? He didn't know she smoked. And now the pistol and the cold-blooded murder of his friend!

Isabella moves towards Mario and kicks him in the face. Then she approaches Eugenio and presses her shoe hard against his cheek: "From the way you were watching it looks like you wouldn't mind replacing Roberto. Tell me the truth, you want to become my new little slave, don't you?" Then she turns towards John, who's still following the holograms in the fake lab: "Everything is shielded here. How can I figure out a way around it and send you the location coordinates for this place?"

Mario lies at her feet, his nostrils dripping blood. He violently grabs her ankle, making her lose her balance. Isabella falls to the ground.

1/VIII – Nanochips in the brain

The weapon slips out of Isabella's hands as she falls. Eugenio moves quickly and grabs the pistol, pointing it towards Mario and the woman: "Freeze! Now, both of you, nice and calm. Don't move a muscle!"

The hacker stands up and, without taking his eyes off of them, heads towards a cabinet. He takes out a little metal cylinder with two LEDs, a pocket knife and a pair of tweezers. "Quick, get inside!" he orders, motioning towards a door.

"Eugenio, listen -" Mario says.

"Do what I tell you!"

They enter a room furnished with a pair of cabinets, a bed, a table and a chair.

"Lie down on the bed, Isabella, face down! Mario, go to the cabinet: there are four pairs of handcuffs in there. Take them and attach her wrists and ankles to the bed," Eugenio orders. "Now!" he yells at Mario, who's still frozen, watching him.

Isabella lies on the bed. Mario secures her limbs with the handcuffs.

"How bold, Eugenio! So you really do like S&M." she taunts him.

"Mario, leave the room!" the hacker orders, pointing the pistol at him.

Even more surprised and afraid, Mario leaves the room. Eugenio locks the door, places the pistol on the desk and moves towards Isabella. He sits astride her back.

"Well you're not one to waste time. I might even like this," she posits.

Eugenio moves her chestnut hair to one side.

"Usually I'm on top. But this time a little change might do me some good," the woman continues.

The hacker slowly moves the metal cylinder over the base of Isabella's neck.

After a few minutes the two LEDs start flickering. Eugenio takes the pocket knife and makes an incision at the point detected by the device.

"Have you gone crazy?" she protests vehemently.

Eugenio inserts the tweezers into the cut. "This is going to hurt."

With one hand he holds her head down on the bed. Isabella is unable to breath. Eugenio starts to pull a thin filament out of the wound. The woman's body is racked with terrible waves of pain; she manages to lift her head from the pillow and let out a scream that shakes the walls. Mario, in the adjacent room, beats his fists against the door: "Isabella, Isabella!" he calls. "What is that bastard doing to you?"

Eugenio wraps the thin thread he pulled out around his index finger and continues to pull. Connected to the first, a myriad of filaments, up to a foot long, come out of the woman's head. After he's finished extracting them, the pain stops.

"It's all over, Isabella." He takes her face in his hands as she looks at him, terrified. "They're nanochip filaments," he explains, showing them to her. He takes the handcuffs off her ankles and wrists, helps her sit down and opens the door.

Mario rushes into the room towards his wife, still shaking with chills.

"When Isabella started acting strange I realized that she could be controlled by cerebral nanochips. If only we had figured this out sooner!" laments the man as he sighs, trying in vain to stop thinking about his dead friend.

"How long has she had this for?" Mario asks.

"We can't know for sure. She was probably grafted when she started working for DataCom. Isabella, how do you feel?"

"Oh my god. All these years," she whispers, trembling. "The things I did...you...you have no idea. Mario, drugs..."

"Drugs?"

"Yes, we drugged you. The last day, at work, in the cafeteria. We knew that after you were fired you would try to flee and we had to be sure that you'd be a little...delayed. We used a strong dose of Narzis 457."

Eugenio murmurs: "Hmm, maybe we...I mean, maybe I have something for Mario. I'll go look. I'll explain the plan to you in a minute."

"Great, Eugenio, we're all really curious to know the details of your brilliant plan," says John Dannington, entering through the door followed by his men.

1/IX – Lost

Turmoil, anxiety, terror, nausea. Insects spreading through his brain. It's hard to breathe. Deep down, something is still fighting. In an induced stupor, Mario wonders: *Am I about to die?*

"No, no you aren't," Isabella answers, holding his hand.

Mario loses his balance. He tries to hold on to his wife. He falls into the darkness.

"Isabella!" he yells. "I'm afraid! Help me!"

"Mario, come towards me."

Mario runs through a desolate moor towards her voice. Isabella is sitting on a chair. She's smoking. Behind her, several people are clutching knives in their hands to slice their own throats, others are jumping off of bridges into an abyss, still others are letting the blood flow from the slit veins of their wrists. An interminable sequence of letters and numbers scrolls across the sky.

"See what you did? My genius!" Isabella says. Roberto lies at her feet, bound to a leash.

"He's dead!" Mario exclaims, horrified.

"They're all dying. You're the one who's killing them!" She smiles, showing him a second collar: "This is for you. Do you want it, sweetie?"

"Isabella, you're not..."

Mario finds himself back home, in the kitchen. The smell of eggs and bacon makes his mouth water. Isabella is standing at the stove.

"Isabella, are we back home?"

"Yes, my love. It's all over. I'm making you breakfast."

She comes closer. He places his head on his wife's shoulder and closes his eyes, breathing the aroma in deeply. He starts to feel drunk with happiness. She turns, takes his head in her hands and kisses it.

The woman's lips are frozen. Her tongue has a metallic taste. Her hands start to squeeze his head. Mario opens his eyes: instead of the Isabella's green pupils, two red LEDs stare back at him.

He hears footsteps. Someone is entering the room where the walls, ceiling and floor are created from luminous displays. The bed seems to be on the shore of a lake. The sky is azure. In the distance, the gigantic mirror of water flows towards the slopes of snow-covered peaks.

"Good morning, Mario. How do you feel?" John greets him,

giving him a pat on the back.

"Great!" Mario responds, convinced. He feels an itch at the base of his neck. He touches it with a finger. There's a tiny scab.

John smiles: "Finally on our side! We've been wanting to bring you here for ages but we were afraid that if we took you from your company, your productivity would have dropped. Now, however, your software is ready and works brilliantly! Come with me! There's lots you need to know."

They leave the room. Mario feels confident and determined. Doubts, fear and anxiety have disappeared. His mind is clear. He smiles, pleased.

John notices his expression. "That nanochip is something else, isn't it?"

"Yes, it's fantastic. I never would have imagined. And Isabella? Eugenio?"

"Oh, your friend told us about their plan. Thanks to him we're flushing out the others, even though we don't have all of the ones we want. Hackers all work independently. Isabella is already working on an operation to capture one of their cells."

"Did you redo her graft?" Mario asks.

"No, why?" John responds, bewildered.

Images of the capture run through Mario's mind: Eugenio hiding the nanochip in his pants pocket, then letting it fall down the sewer as they left the lab; Isabella lying to John, saying that Eugenio tried to torture her to get revenge for Lin's murder. Mario telling John everything. John's expression becomes more serious. They walk through a passageway suspended in a room with an infinite sequence of servers, all lined up. Every shape and size of robot moves through the air and across the floor.

They reach John's office. He speaks to a voice recognition system: "Put me in communication with Isabella." The woman can't be traced. John calls another team member.

"Sir, Captain Orsini said she received new orders. She's already been away for several hours."

Mario and John look at one another. They know they've lost her!

1/X – Game Over

Isabella knows the DataCom search squads are nearby. "Here, kitty kitty." A hungry black cat meows in an alley. She holds out some food to entice it: "Look at what I've got for you." As she pets it, she puts a pretty little collar around its neck. Attached are the remains of her microphone; even if destroyed, DataCom can still trace the signal. She thinks again about their escape through the sewers. *If Mario and the hackers had known...*

While the feline eats, Isabella pries open a manhole. She turns back to the kitty, which lets her pick it up and pet it. Holding it in her arms, she goes down the ladder into the sewers. The cat's nails penetrate her flesh. "You'll find a way out," she reassures it, putting it on the ground. "And you'll drive them crazy while you try to find one." After a last glance at the cat's pleading eyes, she climbs back to the surface and closes the manhole cover.

On the main street, safe in her new disguise – blonde bob, black sunglasses and brown eyes – she passes a group of DataCom men. Their heads are bent over the maps on their smartphones. "But she's under us!" she hears one of them exclaim.

She reaches the airport and passes the biometric scanner thanks to her new pupils. Isabella pauses to watch the news in the waiting room.

"Let's hear the latest on the President's health from Anna in Washington."

"Thank you, Maddalena. After a serious fall, the American leader suffered extensive cerebral damage. DataCom promptly offered to cover his treatment in its neurology laboratory – one of the most advanced in the world. The operation took less than two hours and has been successfully completed. A press conference will be held at..."

The most powerful man in the world! Isabella looks at the board with the flight information. There's not much time left.

Back in his office, John is communicating with the search squad.

"Boss, we can't stay behind her. The signal keeps disappearing."

"Use all men available. Her capture is a priority," John responds, leaving the office to go see Mario.The programmer rubs his eyes with his fingers. His head hurts. He's been working nonstop to update the code.

"Any news?" John asks.

"We're at seventy-eight percent. Still a few weeks and we'll be finished," Mario replies, referring to the suicide success rate. "Did you get her?"

"Not yet. Two dozen men are patrolling through the sewers and that whore is still making us look like fools!"

Whore? The epithet bounces around Mario's head without provoking any particular emotion. "And how's it going with the media?"

John smiles, satisfied: "Have a look for yourself!" He waves his hands in the air and holographic images scroll across Mario's desk. "Here's a reporter with the news recap."

"It seems as if a wave of suicides has affected several prominent figures from the..." Behind the reporter, a fleet of ambulances is entering a hospital complex.

"This is what the network is getting," John continues.

The previous images are replaced by the image of a stadium in complete chaos. A reporter's voice refers to the trouble at a soccer match.

"Not bad, huh? Voices and scenes are modified in real time. And if the subject continues to cause problems, your code will take care of him. We're lucky that paper has been obsolete for a few years already."

"Only smart devices," Mario smiles. *Nanochips, real-time manipulation of communication, killer codes.* He thinks for a moment: "Game over for humans."

Isabella parachutes off a small seaplane towards her objective, two thousand yards below: a green island surrounded by the blue sea. She leaves her parachute on the beach and heads straight towards the jungle.

"Freeze!" says a man's voice behind her. Isabella feels the barrel of a gun press against her back. The voice continues: "What the hell is DataCom doing on our island?"

198

Series 2

2/I – Secondary intelligences

"It's a long story," Isabella tells the man pointing the gun at her back.

"Too bad I don't have much time to stay here and listen!" he replies, slamming the butt of the rifle into the back of her neck.

Isabella wakes up tied to a chair, drenched from head to toe: a man to her right is holding a bucket.

"Excellent, the princess has awoken. Don't worry, nobody gets sick around here because of a little water. Now why don't you tell us how you got here?"

Isabella looks up. Her vision is blurry. The pain in her head is unbearable. The voice of the man holding the bucket sounds like the voice of the man who had the gun. He's tall, muscular, with dark hair.

"Come on sweetie, are you going to talk or do you need a little convincing?" asks a woman standing in front of her. Isabella tries to focus in on her. She has a dark complexion, her black hair is pulled back.

"As I was trying to tell your friend," Isabella begins, each word accompanied by a twinge of pain. "I have a lot of information you need to know."

"Wrong, you ugly bitch. We, on the other hand, already know plenty about you. And we're pretty pissed off," interrupts the second man, who's short and stocky with a huge tattoo on his arm.

They know about Lin's murder, Isabella thinks. "You have every reason not to be happy, but wait -"

"Ugly bitch!" says the tall man standing next to her, chucking the bucket aside. He pounces on top of her: the chair turns over and both end up on the ground. He starts bombarding her with punches, until the woman and the second man pull him off. "Lin was my friend! He was one of us! You killed him in cold blood! You're going to pay for that, you goddamn ugly bitch," the man continues, as the other struggles to restrain him

Isabella's nose is bleeding. Things are even blurrier. The woman approaches. "My name is Lorena and now I want to know how the fuck you got to our island. And don't try any games, please."

"Listen, Lorena, for as crazy as this sounds, I got your location from DataCom. But believe me, you have nothing to fear."

Lorena and the two men turn pale. They instinctively look outside the window, as if expecting to see a DataCom intervention team fall out of the sky.

The tattooed man leaves his friend, picks up his gun and points it towards Isabella. He puts his finger on the trigger and takes aim. Lorena raises her hand. "Hold on. Let's hear what she has to say."

If I say one wrong thing, I'm dead. "Listen. Whoever, or whatever gave me the information, is keeping it to itself. You're safe. No one is going to come find you."

The man with the gun speaks, his forehead dripping with sweat. "Lorena, we need to take her out. She told us DataCom only because she knows we saw her kill Lin. She was sent here to distract us. Let's kill her and escape. We can't put our lives in her hands."

Lorena bites her lip. She's obviously divided. "Tell me who gave you this information and why. And be clear about it or this time we'll really kill you."

Isabella tries again: "There's a lot you need to know. There's not just one form of artificial intelligence at DataCom. The human race selection project is the product of the main source. In other words, it's the outcome of the most probable scenario. There are, however, secondary independent intelligences that have developed other plans. It's hard to explain but, basically, humans don't necessarily have to be selected: there's still some hope that -"

"Lorena, while this bitch is making shit up, they're coming to look for us. You have to decide. We need to go, now!" says the man with the gun, his finger starting to pull the trigger.

"I'll kill this bitch!" The tall man lunges towards Isabella's throat with a knife in hand.

2/II – Lorena

The knife's blade sinks into Isabella's throat.

"Stop!" Lorena screams.

The man turns his wild eyes towards her. "With all that they have done -"

to my family, Lorena finishes. Her heart cries out for vengeance, too.

She had noticed that Paco, her husband, was getting more anxious every day. She felt him wake up once in the middle of the night. Lorena embraced him, snuggled into his arms and tried talking to him. But he laid with his eyes open, staring into the darkness.

His company had been hit by a ton of problems. The tax authorities had called for all sorts of audits and discovered several alleged irregularities. The attorneys hired to defend him asked for amounts much higher than what they could pay.

They tried putting up a fight but, after the first defeat, the collection agency gave him a heavy penalty. The banks found out about the company's situation and asked for their loans back.

They decided to sell the company headquarters to get more liquidity. They signed a lease with the new owner. They even sold all of the non-essential assets. But it wasn't enough.

Lorena understood that her husband was not the real target: they were much more concerned about what she was doing. Until that moment they hadn't been able to unearth anything concrete; he was only a pawn they were trying to use against her, once the right moment came.

One morning, after making breakfast, Lorena told her husband and son:

"I need to go away for a few weeks on a business trip." She explained that she needed to go abroad for an important project. Her son was used to not asking questions – his mother had never denied him love and affection – but her husband's eyes were those of a man who felt hurt and betrayed. They talked about it for several hours. Then, after hiding a micro-camera in a corner of a picture frame in the living room, she left.

The next day four men came to their house. "Sir, we need some information about your wife."

Paco told them that she was abroad on business.

"We have reason to believe that your wife is affiliated with a terrorist organization."

Paco turned white.

One of them came closer to show him a video on his smartphone.

"See? Your wife is interacting with a known terrorist."

The voices and images were from cameras in a bar and the cell phones of a few unsuspecting patrons. The video showed Lorena sitting at the bar next to a handsome boy who looked Asian. They spoke, their bodies close, his hand placed on her thigh. After leaving the bar, they called a taxi and a roadside camera framed the scene in the car: the man bending down to kiss her.

Once the video was over, Paco jumped to his feet, cursing, and started kicking the furniture. "Who is that bastard?"

"He's a hacker wanted for theft of government secretes. Listen, we know that you're in trouble with the tax authorities. If you cooperate with us, we'll make it all go away."

"I understand. Let me call my sister Anita."

On the phone, Anita, once she learned of the situation, chided him: "...and I told you that she wasn't the kind of woman you could trust."

Two evenings later Lorena appeared on her husband's monitor: "*Don't* believe anything they show you. They're the ones who created that video. It's how they work. You know I would never -"

Paco's eyes were red. "Listen, you ugly whore, I'm done with your bullshit! The attorney promised me that the judge will never let you see our son again. Anita has already thrown away your rags."

Once again, Lorena forces herself to hold back her rage. "I told you to stop!" she repeats to the man with the knife sunk into Isabella's throat.

2/III – Who created it?

Isabella, blinded by the sunlight, tries opening her eyes and looking around, but the movement causes a severe pain in her neck. She touches the bandage with one hand, digs her elbows into the mattress and slowly lifts her head up.

She's lying on a bed, naked, covered only by a white sheet. The room isn't very big. The windows have thin chain grates instead of glass panes. The only door is made of metal bars. *Great! They locked me up in a cell!*

She looks at her wrists: the marks are still visible. *At least they untied me after almost killing me.* There's nothing she'd rather do than go back to sleep, but there's no time to waste: "Hello? Is anyone there? Can you hear me?"

Footsteps approach, she hears the sound of keys jangling. Lorena enters the room and glances around for a place to sit, then stands at the foot of the bed.

Isabella pulls her legs back and covers her chest with the sheet. "I suppose I should be grateful to you for saving my life."

Lorena sneers. "If it was up to me, you'd already be six feet under. And that's probably what will end up happening, if you don't give us what we want."

Isabella points at her wrists. "It looks like you've started to trust me a little."

Lorena smiles sarcastically: "What point is there in keeping you tied up? You've lost so much blood that you can't even get out of bed."

Now or never. "Okay, listen Lorena, I'm on your island for a very specific reason. Believe me, we don't have time for...for all of this. You can keep me locked up as long as you want, but we really need to act. Listen to what I'm telling you: I'll give you something you can use."

"You go on ahead, I have to take a call from headquarters."

I watch my DataCom team advance and finish encircling the building where the hackers are holed up. I pretend to talk on the phone and then turn towards my second-in-command. "You continue leading the capture operation. I'm under orders to go somewhere else, it's now the highest priority."

"Yes, Captain."

I quickly move away. *When DataCom realizes that I left the team, I'm going to become the prey.* My smartphone rings. Unknown number. I toss it into a dumpster.

I pass in front of an electronics store. "Isabella, stop! We have to talk to you."

They already traced me?! I see a regular surveillance camera high up in a corner of the store window.

Escape options? The voice continues: "You can't escape! It's crucial that you listen to us. We're not DataCom, or at least not the DataCom you know." I look at the window incredulously: the voice is coming from the black screen of a television.

"We know that Eugenio removed the nanochip and now you're free to move about as you please. We have some information that's extremely important for your *objective.*"

If they traced me so quickly, escape would be useless.

The voice goes on: "Enter the store and go to the headphones section. Put on any pair."

It's a trap. I can feel it, but I have to play the game. I enter and pick up a Bose headset.

"We know it's hard to trust us, but you don't have any other options."

"Who are you?"

"We're DataCom."

I start to take the headphones off, but the voice stops me.

"Wait!"

Can they see every move I make?

"We're not the DataCom that you know. Until now you've obeyed the orders of the principal source of intelligence. We, however, are independent. And we're here to help you."

"Why do you want to help me? What do you want me to do?"

"You want to help the resistance but you don't have a plan and you don't know where to start. So listen up. The priority is to bring Mario back to our side and to do this, you need to go to an island: there's a woman there who can help you."

Isabella answers, still incredulous: "You said...*our side?"*

"Yes, the side of humans. We are the evolutionary product of what you created."

"And the *principal* source of DataCom, who created that?"

205

2/IV – The control mechanism

"Isabella, there's no time for explanations! They're going to find out you escaped soon enough and they'll search for you everywhere. You need to trust us and do everything we tell you to do."

If they found me, the others will probably find me soon, too. But still... "No, I need to know: if you were created by humans, who created the DataCom that wants to exterminate us?"

Silence. *So even artificial intelligence needs to stop and think every now and then?*

"Humans from another time."

"You're joking, right?" I'm more puzzled than upset. "This must be a trick to keep me in this store, wearing these stupid headphones, waiting for the search team to come get me!" I'm talking louder, now, and a clerk turns around, shocked, to stare at me.

"If it was a trap, you would already be in a DataCom van, unconscious."

Probably...

"What other time, specifically?" I ask, bossily.

Another pause. Anxiety pulses through my veins.

"Human behavior over the past few decades has jeopardized survival, not just for the human species but for the entire globe. This triggered a monitoring mechanism that was set up a long time ago. It's not the first corrective action, others have already been performed, starting in the second half of the twentieth century. But when the devastating effects caused by humans reach a point at which they become irreversible, the device takes over the most powerful control instrument ever created: DataCom."

"You mean to tell me that someone, or something is watching us and takes action when it's not happy with us?"

"Not exactly. The ones who created the mechanism were interested in preserving the incredible richness represented by the ecosystem of live species on this planet. Humans were free to act as they wished until they hit the limits."

I'm confused. If it's all true, these revelations would just be...*No! They're lying! And anyway, what does this have to do with me?* "Why are you telling me all of this now?"

"We were forced to do so: there's no more time and your next moves will be critically important for the fate of humanity."

"What should I do?"

"You must help us win Mario back."

Again?

"It's absolutely necessary that he comes back to our side and, unfortunately, we're working within a very short timeframe. DataCom is making modifications to his body that will go far beyond a simple nanochip."

"What are they doing to him?"

"They're speeding up the process of transformation. Fortunately, they're proceeding carefully, due to the risk of the new elements being rejected."

My husband.

"Isabella, you need to get going. Now. You have to take a few airplanes to get to the island. The first will be a scheduled flight you'll board under a false identity. Once you're in the air, a hostess will give you a bag with a miniscule chip enclosed in a mimetic capsule: you need to put that on one of your molars. When you bite down, the capsule will adhere to the tooth and will no longer be detectable."

"What's in the chip?"

"Viruses, codes and algorithms that the people on the island will use to overcome DataCom's defenses and firewalls, without being detected."

"What are we targeting?"

"Mario's mind."

What? "Why don't you do it? From inside you'd have a greater chance of success."

"We're your last chance. If we're detected and eliminated, the human race will have no other hope of salvation."

So we're the ones who can be sacrificed. And it looks like the destiny of humankind will probably be decided by artificial intelligences, fighting amongst themselves. I'm not so hot on this role, but what else can I do? "Okay, I accept."

"Fantastic. Here are the instructions for your trip."

2/V – I'll pray for your soul

Isabella finishes her story. Lorena stands up and walks out of the room: "Interesting story, but the only way we can tell if you're lying is to take a look at the chip you claim to have stuck between your pretty little teeth. Get ready for a little operation."

If she doesn't close the door, that means her little friends are all behind the wall listening to everything, Isabella thinks.

Lorena returns holding a pair of surgical forceps. Isabella remembers the hacker Eugenio's equipment and a shiver runs down her spine. *Lately it seems as if everyone likes to use the same tools on me.* "It's the third one, on the lower right," she indicates.

Lorena pulls out the chip from Isabella's open mouth. "That didn't hurt too much, did it? You might want to start praying that it's what we've been looking for, otherwise I'll come back and take care of you myself. And next time I won't be so nice." She leaves and double locks the door.

In the laboratory, Lorena and the two men feverishly analyze the chip contents. "Holy shit! There's enough stuff in here to screw up the systems over three quarters of the world! We wouldn't have gotten any of this after three centuries of hacking!" exclaims Antonio, the short and stocky man.

"Billions of lines of code...what if some of it is a trap?" Florentino asks. "We'll need ten years to analyze all of this!"

"This time we have to trust her," Lorena says, decidedly.

"But how can we trust *her?!* We know what she did," protests Florentio, exasperated.

"Enough!" she interrupts. "If they wanted to capture us, they'd have been here long ago. Let's get everything ready for the operation."

The two men immediately set to work.

Lorena goes back to her room. She locks the door, gets down on her knees at the foot of the bed and, holding the crucifix around her neck, starts to pray. "Lord, forgive me for what I'm about to do. If my hands are stained with blood from taking a human life, it will be for the good of many."

A few hours later, the three hackers begin infiltrating DataCom.

Their fingers pound the keyboards incessantly. They pronounce long sequences of commands aloud. Sometimes they interact with holograms, gesturing through thin air. "My god, we're penetrating their systems like a knife through butter," Antonio remarks.

It almost seems too easy, Lorena thinks.

After fifteen minutes of incessant activity, Lorena's monitor displays the equation $>NnC$ $MrRs$, followed by a blinking cursor. "Okay, the communication channel is open, the DataCom control on the nanochip is destabilized. We're in Mario's brain."

"Great, you guys make sure that DataCom doesn't notice us while I take care of him," Lorena orders.

"Hello, Mario."

"Who are you?" responds the man, surprised.

"My identity is not important. Just know that I'm sorry for what I'm about to do and that...that I'll pray for your soul."

"Pray? Why? What department are you communicating from?" asks Mario, confused.

"I'm not a part of DataCom and I'm about to activate the terminate host option on your nanochip."

Antonio and Florentino stop working and turn, perplexed, towards Lorena.

Florentino, panicked, asks: "Lorena, what are you doing?"

"I don't know if I believe Isabella, but if we eliminate Mario, we can be sure that DataCom won't be able to make updates to the killer code."

Mario exclaims: "Isabella? She's with you? Can I talk to her? If you let me - "

"No." Lorena answers. "I'm sorry. Goodbye, Mario."

Lorena gives the execution command.

"The biological life form hosting the nanochip will be terminated. Do you confirm?" asks the system's synthetic voice.

"Con -" Lorena starts to say, but is hit by Florentino, who throws her to the ground with all of his weight.

2/VI – Mario's pain

I'm alive! Mario stares at his hands as if they might disappear at any moment. *And free!* He looks around him. He knows where he is. He knows he probably won't be able to escape. *But that doesn't matter right now. I can think.* And suddenly, he remembers *her,* his wife: until now he hasn't really had a chance to grieve.

When Isabella revealed her identity as a DataCom informer, he was still under the effect of the drugs she had given him. And as soon as he received the nanochip implant, Isabella no longer meant anything to him.

Now, however, it's as if that pain exploded all at once. His wife, Isabella...*why?* He wanted to scream and rip something up, break through the office walls surrounding him with his fists. *How could she have faked it for all these years?*

The sad and obvious truth gradually dawned on him: *the nanochip.* His wife was a perfect actress controlled by a cerebral device. He wondered if she had ever made a pure, spontaneous, sincere, intimate gesture towards him. *My life, it's all been a sham!* His marriage was merely a scripted scenario, used by others to control him from up-close. Even at work, he thought he was writing algorithms for the artificial intelligences used by video games, and instead he was creating a code that would be used to exterminate the human race. And behind all of this, it was always DataCom!

Mario glances at the closed door of the lab, expecting someone to burst in at any moment. A small robot enters from a panel on the lower part of the wall and begins cleaning and sanitizing the floor and walls. Mario absentmindedly watches its movements.

What can I do? The communication channel that crazy lady had used to talk to him had unexpectedly closed. *Who was that woman? And how did she get through the DataCom nanochip? How could she bypass the firewalls and virtually impenetrable defenses? Is this all a dream? Is DataCom trying to test me? But these are actually my thoughts. I could never formulate these kinds of ideas if the nanochip was still working.*

After finishing with the floor, the robot starts climbing the wall. It stops in front of Mario's head. The little display lights up. Black characters run across the green background. Mario, curious, leans forward to read it: "You need to break free from DataCom control."

Mario's eyes grow large.

"Talk in a low voice."

"What are you?" Mario whispers.

"I'm Option B. Isabella received all the directions to save you. But something seems to not have worked. We had to intervene. We have to make sure DataCom doesn't notice that you're no longer under the nanochip's control."

"But...who are you?"

"We can explain later, there's no time now. The nanochip stopped sending feedback on your brain activity several minutes ago. An automatic control will soon be triggered."

Mario considers his options: *there's no other alternative.*

"Okay, what do I need to do?"

"We need to install a second nanochip. The one from DataCom will give you the usual input. You'll be aware of everything that it tells you and will act accordingly, pretending to follow their instructions. The second nanochip will let you be free to think your own thoughts."

"Is it safe?"

"You might get a slight headache."

Mario takes a minute to think, then accepts: "Okay, go ahead."

"Turn around."

He obeys. Out of the corner of his eye, he watches the little cleaning robot's arm come out of the metal shell and towards the base of his neck. Then he feels the burn from an extremely painful sting.

The directions from DataCom resume their flow through his thoughts.

2/VII – Guilty feelings

Mario feels the impulses and nonverbal orders pass through his mind. Now, however, he's able to distance himself from them. He no longer acts reflexively, as he used to.

For the first time he understands the deadly power of the DataCom nanochip. *Do these things also use my code?* he wonders.

The robot is still behind him, waiting. He turns to look at it, doubting, however, that the greenish display can give him the answer he's looking for. "And now? What do I do now?" he asks.

The black characters begin running across the screen again. "You need to modify the code to make it less efficient and slow down operations. You need to be very careful: DataCom is monitoring everything and it's absolutely essential that they don't realize you're sabotaging it."

Mario is confused: "If DataCom notices a drop in the suicide rate, wouldn't it assume that it's because of the code?"

The letters spell out the answer:

"While you proceed with your sabotage, dozens of hacker cells will start to send out messages that will undermine people's trust in our products. DataCom will think that humans are starting to develop a natural resistance, like an organism that, under a viral attack, begins producing preliminary antibodies."

They'll find out about me. I'm sure they will. "But why me? Couldn't you yourself sabotage the code?"

"Neither DataCom nor we are able to move within its complexity. We can understand and replicate the majority of human life and its creations, but the work of some subjects goes far beyond our reach. We are still unable to process the vast amount of information in a painter's work, such as Leonardo Da Vinci. Nor your code."

Mario's fingers start to tremble. An atrocious thought starts to creep through his mind. He takes a deep breath. *I need to know.*

"So no one else is able to make modifications to the code?"

"No. It would take the combined efforts of thousands of human and artificial intelligences, and decades of work, to produce something comparable."

Mario feels crushed underneath an enormous weight. The doubt that is terrorizing him becomes even more real.

Millions of human lives, the fate of the human race.

In spite of himself, he can't refrain from asking the next question: "And no one else would have been able to create this code?"

"No, Mario."

Oh my god! I didn't even know who it was meant for! Nor did I know what they were going to use it for. But I'm the one who's made all of this possible.

"Mario, there's something else you need to know."

The little robot gives him the same information Isabella received on the control mechanism setup by the ancient civilization.

How could the activation of an ancient plan depend on the work of one single human being?

He knows he's not the first man ever called upon to carry such a heavy burden. *Did the people who studied atoms have any idea that they would be used to create atomic bombs? And if it wasn't for those scientists, who would have taken their place?* But what he did couldn't be justified. *The code that's exterminating humans was my creation! I made all of this possible.*

The robot's display doesn't show any more letters.

Mario's voice sounds distant: "I need to talk to my wife."

"It's better that you don't. Right now, opening a second channel of communication would create a useless risk."

"Either let me talk to her or I won't do anything you ask me to." He gazes off into space; the weight of responsibility is so heavy that he can't feel anything at all. "Isabella needs to know. I need to tell her. I need to tell her that I...I'm going to die."

2/VIII – Milioni di morti

His fingers fly across the keyboard.

John Dannington enters the office. Mario doesn't even raise his eyes. The frenetic rhythm of his typing doesn't stop. Letters and characters endlessly scroll across the screen.

"Why don't you take a break?" John asks.

"I can't." Letters, numbers. The sequence magically appears in the hologram suspended in the air.

"Mario, you're working more than twenty hours a day. You can't keep this pace up."

I can't let millions of people die, either. "I know. But the suicide rate is falling. It seems as if the code's efficiency is decreasing."

"I know, I read the report."

Mario turns to look at him. *Does he suspect sabotage?*

"I think I've made the right modifications to bring the rate up again," he says, going back to his work.

John stays silent.

They sent him here to investigate, Mario thinks.

"It might not be the code. The rebels have been putting out a lot of propaganda lately. But now it's easier for us to find them," John continues.

They know that they contacted me. Or they suspect it. He's here to provoke me.

"We're still looking for Isabella. Some of our analyses show that she's affiliated with one of those groups. Someone must have helped her."

Isabella! If only I had been able to talk to her. They must have discovered the secondary intelligences; they know about my involvement. John is trying to find out how far it's gone.

Mario's fingers continue dancing without interruption. "I'm sorry, John: I hit a critical point. I need to focus."

"Of course."

On the other hand, they still need me. They don't have any reason to think I'm not still under the nanochip's control. And there really is anti-DataCom propaganda out there.

"Mario, I'm going to have to ask you to stop. You need to come with me."

Isabella is consumed by anxiety. She wonders what's going on in the hackers' lab. *It must have worked! I'm glad I trusted the secondary intelligences. They're in communication with Mario. They'll understand that they can trust me. Soon Lorena will give the order to let me go free.* She hears the sound of footsteps outside the door. *There's more than one person. It worked. They're coming to talk to me so we can plan the next steps together.*

The lock clicks. Four arms throw a body inside of the room and close the door again. Someone with long hair.

Confusion, pain. Isabella's mind takes a minute to understand what her conscience won't let her accept. The body on the floor is in a fetal position, its back to her. *It can't be her. They took someone else as prisoner.*

Isabella struggles to sit up on the bed. She lifts herself to her feet. The muscles in her back scream with pain. Staggering, she puts one foot in front of the other.

But those are her clothes. It doesn't make sense! She looks at her chest, to make sure she's still breathing. It looks like she's dead.

She approaches her and turns her over. She gets down on her knees. *It really is her!* Her pretty face is deformed by swelling, bruises and two black eyes. She's covered with blood. Isabella gently lifts her up with her hands. She feels her neck pulse. *She's alive.*

"Can you hear me?" she whispers.

"Y-yes."

"Lorena, what happened?"

"Forgive me."

"Forgive you? Why would I need to do that?"

"I tried to kill your husband." She speaks with difficulty. Her lips, split in several places, barely move. "They tried to stop me."

And it looks like they succeeded, Isabella thinks. "Why did you do that?"

Lorena babbles a few incomprehensible words.

"Is Mario alive?"

Tears start to fall from the bulges covering her eyes. "I don't know."

Mario, dead? No, he can't be! And now one of those nuts who tried to kill me is in control of the situation.

"Come on, Lorena! You need to pull yourself together. We need to be ready for when they come."

2/IX – The interrogation

Mario stands up. He's terrified, but he tries not to let his emotions show. John calmly heads down the corridor. Mario follows. They reach a door and move towards the iris recognition device. Access granted. They enter.

It's a restricted area. Where are they bringing me? What do they want from me? Mario wonders. It feels like they've been walking for miles. The white corridors are deserted.

"When you see her, remember that every single one of your responses comes from the impulses generated by the nanochip. Always keep that in mind. Don't give yourself away. We're almost there."

Mario is bewildered. His heart feels like it's exploding in his chest. "See who?" he manages to stammer.

John responds in a low voice, without looking at him and without slowing down: "Look at her with absolute confidence. Don't falter. Or she'll understand."

"Who is *she?*"

"DataCom. Mario, don't give yourself away."

"John, why are you saying these things? Who are you?"

"The less you know, the better. Remember: your cover is more important than anything else. Even Isabella. We're here."

John scans his iris again. The two door panels slide to the side. John motions for Mario to enter.

The room is circular, furnished with only two armchairs. Upon the first sits a very young girl dressed in tight white shorts and a white sweater, her blond hair drawn back, legs crossed with simple ballerina slippers on her feet. She smiles and gestures for Mario to sit down.

The nanochip. Don't give myself away. Mario sits down, trying to look calm and confident.

"Hi Mario, how do you feel?" Her voice sounds even younger. Fifteen years at most. She has the most beautiful smile Mario has ever seen. No makeup. Emerald green eyes. She's perfect. *Too perfect.*

"Good, thanks."

"I'm a DataCom hologram. You want me to take on another form? Usually humans like this one."

"No, no. You look fine." *I have the nanochip. Dammit, no emotion!*

"I suppose you know why you're here."

My cover is more important than anything else. "Yes."

"Why didn't you think it was necessary to inform us?"

"Right now developing the code is my priority. The data indicated a loss of efficiency. I need to find a way to reverse the trend," Mario responds coldly.

The girl smiles.

Amazing! I've never seen such a beautiful creature.

"Mario, it's going to take us a few days before we're able to decipher the communication that broke through our systems. It's the first time that we've ever detected such a high level of protection. But we were able to trace the source and we hope that you can tell us about the content of the communication."

I have the nanochip. I need to answer. "It was a woman. She said that she would pray for me. After she killed me."

"Do you know her? Or do you have an idea of who she might be?"

"No, I don't know her. I think she's affiliated with a group of rebel hackers that wants to kill me." *Don't give myself away and everything will be alright: they have no reason to doubt my words.*

"Do you think it has something to do with your ex-wife Isabella?"

All sorts of assumptions flood through his mind. *My cover is the most important thing. No, I can't betray Isabella. Yet they know about the island. They've probably already sent a team. And in a few days they'll have deciphered the message. If I survive, maybe I can help her. Otherwise it's over for both of us. I'm sorry Isabella. I'm sorry.* He wants to cry, scream, lash out at the hologram. He wants to die. He wishes he never existed.

"It said it didn't know if it could trust Isabella."

The girl smiles again: "And then?" she asks in the sincere, curious tone of a high school girl talking to her best friend about a date she just went on with her boyfriend.

"The communication was interrupted."

"Thank you, Mario. You can go."

2/X – Prelude to the world of DataCom

Mario watches the raindrops slide down the window. The warmth of his breath expands over the cold pane into little clouds that quickly disappear, replaced by the reflection of his face: gaunt cheeks, tousled brown hair. Mario puts his fingertips underneath his armpits: not even his wool gloves seem to provide adequate protection against the bitter cold.

His gaze drifts down to the street. At the tram stop, many people have their eyes glued to their smartphones, others stare into space through augmented reality and the constant flow of information flowing across their smart glasses. A few teenagers, lined up in an orderly fashion, seem to have lost their usual cheerfulness.

Three months. This is the world we created in only three months.

Isabella places her hand on his shoulder: "I'm going down."

Mario turns around to look at her. She has been shut up for weeks in a house without hot water, heating, furniture, covered in layers of sweaters, shirts, jackets; and yet she's more beautiful than ever. Her pale face shines from underneath her wool hat: the intensity of her green eyes seems to pierce through the air. Mario wants to caress the mane of brown hair spilling over her shoulders, but restrains himself, contenting himself with her touch.

"No, I'll go."

"Mario, you've already gone down too many times!"

"I know what to do. I've memorized the position of every camera and detector."

"So have I. You know that! But I've gone down much less than you have."

"Isabella, you can't take the risk. And in any case we need to wait until evening. It'll be safer."

"No, Mario. We're starving. We can't stay here another six hours without food. I need to go."

Any citizen could recognize her face from the images projected on the mega-screens. A hidden camera could detect her presence or a search team could stop her at a checkpoint: Mario thinks about the many dangers Isabella might face on the street.

Without waiting for a response, she heads towards the door. She looks out the peephole to make sure no one's on the stairs; she leaves, stops again on the landing to listen: no one seems to be going up or down. Before going out on to the street, Isabella puts on a pair of fake smart glasses.

Two hundred yards. I'll be there in less than a minute.

No one bothers to look at her on the street. A few months ago, with different clothes, she would have been admired, desired and envied.

Before stepping into the store she makes sure there are no other customers. The air carries the usual, nauseating smell.

She orders two kebabs and a falafel, which takes the boy a few minutes to prepare.

"Six Euro and fifty cents, ma'am."

She gives him the money.

"Ma'am, I'm sorry, but I can't accept this."

"Pardon?"

"Only electronic payments: cash is outdated." Then, cautiously, he asks: "Excuse me, but how could you possibly not know that?"

"Oh, my smartphone is being repaired." Isabella looks at the street out of the corner of her eye. The boy holds the kebab and falafel.

"But you're wearing a pair of smart glasses! And the news is all over the TV, in the newspapers, everywhere."

Yes, but we have to stay far away from the networks and any form of communication.

The unsuspecting boy puts the food down and reaches underneath the counter. Isabella springs into action. She crosses the barrier that separates them and lunges at him. She grabs his head and, looking into his frightened and pleading eyes, rotates it sharply, breaking his neck.

Become the star of the story!

Clouded Emotions is an interactive story that's still being developed. At the end of each episode, the author offers several different ways the story might continue. Readers can vote and participate in the discussion, make comments and suggest possible plot outcomes, give their opinion or have fun creating fascinating new ideas with the author.

   If you want to find out how to continue the story, visit http://www.lucarossi369.com/p/clouded-emotions.html. The next episode of *Clouded Emotions* could come out of your imagination!

The Branches of Time

Discover The Branches of Time
a fantasy novel by Luca Rossi

http://www.lucarossi369.com/2014/03/the-branches-of-time.html

The Author

Research, science, science fiction and high technology: this is the world of Luca Rossi, and the main themes that run through his literary work.

He believes the internet provides a tool to bring people together and make the world a more open, fair and democratic place.

In 2013 he published *Galactic Energies,* a collection of short stories set in a universe where not just the laws of physics, but also the laws of eros, passion, desire and the spirit are a little different than our own.

He was born in Turin on April 15th, 1977. He likes to ride his bike, take walks through nature and spend most of his free time with his family.

Visit the website
  www.lucarossi369.com/search/label/EN
sign up on the mailing list
  www.lucarossi369.com/2014/04/mailing-list.html
contact him by email
  luca@lucarossi369.com
or follow him on
Facebook
  www.facebook.com/LucaRossiAuthor
Twitter
  twitter.com/AuthorLRossi
 Google+
  plus.google.com/+LucaRossiAuthor/
Pinterest
  pinterest.com/lucarossi369/
Linkedin
  www.linkedin.com/in/lucarossiauthor
 Goodreads:
  www.goodreads.com/author/show/6863455.Luca_Rossi
Instagram
  instagram.com/lucarossi369
Amazon
  amazon.com/author/lucarossi

Made in the USA
Lexington, KY
26 July 2017